Author dedication:
To Mum and Dad, for making me a writer

Monstrum House: Sucked Under
published in 2010 by
Hardie Grant Egmont
85 High Street
Prahran, Victoria 3181, Australia
www.hardiegrantegmont.com.au

A CiP record for this title is available from the National Library of Australia.

Text copyright © 2010 Zana Fraillon
Illustration and design copyright © 2010 Hardie Grant Egmont

Design and illustration by Simon Swingler
Typeset by Ektavo

Printed in Australia by McPherson's Printing Group

1 3 5 7 9 10 8 6 4 2

Sucked Under

By Zana Fraillon

Illustrations by Simon Swingler

hardie grant EGMONT

Jasper McPhee pulled himself over the top of the icy wall. He landed lightly on his bare feet and rolled across the snowy ground, just dodging the swinging blades that whooshed from the tree tops. *That was close,* he thought. He shot a quick look at his watch. He had two minutes left to finish the combat course. He might just make it.

Only one more stretch of ground to go, then he had to get past the mud and up the rope. He commando-crawled quickly through the snow, keeping his head down and eyes up, like he'd been taught. One minute left …

Jasper leapt over the seething pile of mud, trying not to think of all the things that could be in there. Their teacher Sir Tavish had told them that it was infested with Midgiemunches, but Jasper hoped he wasn't serious. After all, the venom in a Midgiemunch was strong enough to paralyse a small child.

Jasper sprang upwards to catch hold of the swinging rope. Twenty seconds to go …

I'm actually going to make it! Jasper thought. *No penalty points!* He almost whooped with glee. The kids who didn't finish the course in time were given ten penalty points. Twenty penalty points meant getting a punishment, and in the last year Jasper had earnt himself enough punishments to last a lifetime.

Jasper swung confidently over the icy lake

and landed firmly on the bank, just as Sir Tavish's bugle sounded. Time was up.

There was a groan from the students who were still doing the course. Jasper's friend Felix had only just reached the rope. Felix shook his head as he collected a penalty card from Sir Tavish, and made his way over to Jasper.

Saffy joined the boys, looking smug at having finished the course before both Felix and Jasper – again. It annoyed both boys that they were constantly being beaten through the combat course by a girl – even if she was a girl who could easily destroy both of them in a kickboxing contest.

Of all the classes at Monstrum House, Combative Calculations was Jasper's favourite. Each class was a huge obstacle course, and the stunts they learnt were brilliant. The best one so far was learning how to flip off a high ledge and land so it didn't even hurt. It was just like being a stuntman in an action film. The only bad thing about Combative Calculations was that Sir Tavish always made them stand barefoot in the snow at the end of class while he told them how they could improve.

'A'RIGH'! LEF' FEET! NOW!' Sir Tavish bellowed.

Everyone balanced on one bare foot on the icy ground. They had done this every day for almost a year now, so no-one thought it was unusual anymore. Freezing your feet in the snow was the only way to stop your brain from shrinking. The students at Monstrum House had been warned about brain shrinkage. According to their principal, most adults had brains the size of prunes. A shrunken brain meant that you couldn't see monsters anymore. And if you couldn't see monsters, you were in trouble.

Sir Tavish

Flaming red hair

Blow through the other end

'Tha' was pathetic,' Sir Tavish yelled.

Jasper rolled his eyes. Sir Tavish gave this speech at the end of every class. It had taken the students a while to realise that if Sir Tavish *didn't* single you out, you were doing well.

'Ye, McPhee,' Sir Tavish turned, 'Din't ye even nootice the flyin' Scramblers when ye flipped o'er the wall?'

Jasper glanced at Felix. *There were flying Scramblers?* 'Um, well ...' Jasper muttered.

'PATHETIC! Ye need to watch for more than one monstar! Doon't ye know tha' monstars doon't always go it aloone? They can team oop and git ye twice as good! Change feet!'

The students dutifully swapped feet as Sir Tavish walked up and down the line, singling out students to yell at. Saffy, as usual, didn't get a mention.

'Now, I want two lines nex' teh each other.

Be quick aboot it,' Sir Tavish ordered.

Jasper looked curiously at Felix. This was new.

'Look a' the person nex' teh ye,' Sir Tavish said.

Jasper made a stupid face at Felix, who choked back a laugh.

'Somethin' teh say, Mr Brown?' Sir Tavish asked. 'Or are ye just laughin' because ye're stuck with McPhee for yer nex' test?'

The students had never done a test in pairs before. *Cool*, Jasper thought. He glanced behind him. Saffy was paired with Callum, a small kid from their class. Saffy would be happy – Callum was easily the best student at Combative Calculations.

'Sorry, mate,' Jasper whispered to Felix. 'Let's just hope it's not an important test.'

Felix grinned in response. Jasper knew they

would actually team up pretty well together.

'Head back noow. Stenka is waitin' to show ye teh ye test rooms. It's a test on Morphers, so keep ye wits aboot ye. We don't have tha' much anti-venom on hand.'

Jasper hoped Sir Tavish was joking. 'How can they be running out of anti-venom?' he whispered to Felix.

'Um, let's see now …' said Felix. 'Could it be because this is a monster-hunting school and kids get Monstered, like, every single day?'

'Good point,' said Jasper. 'But it's just a test, right? I reckon they'd stop it if you were in real trouble. That's what they always do in tests.'

Sir Tavish's voice boomed across their conversation. 'Hurry up, ye two!' he yelled. 'This test ain't like no other ye've doone!'

'There goes that theory,' Felix grimaced.

The headphones in the test room were broken. Definitely broken. The high-pitched beeping was beginning to get annoying. Jasper gave the headphones one last tap before ripping them off his head.

He looked around the dark room for any sign of a monster. His eyes were stinging. His head was aching. *Maybe I'm getting a cold from standing in the stupid snow so much,* he thought distractedly. He was finding it hard to concentrate. *Test. Think about the test,* he reminded himself.

Jasper heard something shuffling around in the room. Something clumsy. It grunted as it walked right into a wall.

Silently, Jasper pulled the net from his hunt belt. He could just make out a figure in the far corner of the room. It was about the same size as him. *Too easy*, thought Jasper, raising the net.

A small doubt niggled at the back of Jasper's brain. The figure edged slightly to the right. Jasper knew that if he waited, it could all go wrong. He shook the doubt from his head, ran towards the figure and swung his net.

The next thing Jasper knew, his legs were kicked out from underneath him and he thumped onto the floor. Not *exactly* how monster-hunting was meant to go. *At least I've got the monster*, thought Jasper. He grabbed the torch from his hunt belt and switched it on.

'Felix?' Jasper whispered. His friend stood

tangled in the net.

'Where are we?' asked Felix.

Jasper shook his head. 'We're in a test, aren't we? But what are you doing here? You're not meant to be here, are you?' He shivered and pulled his hood up. It was *cold*.

'Why am I in a net?' Felix scratched his head.

Jasper shrugged and shone the torch around the room. *Where are we?*

Jasper could feel an idea trying to burst through his skull, desperately wanting to be heard.

He shone the torch directly in Felix's eyes. Felix blinked and looked around the room, as if trying to get his bearings. Jasper saw something purple flash inside Felix's ear, then disappear.

He felt a tingle of excitement in the tips of his fingers. Without really knowing why, he tackled Felix to the ground.

11

Felix struggled hopelessly in the net.

'Stay still!' yelled Jasper.

He grabbed the ear plunger – which looked like a mini toilet-plunger – from his hunt belt and shoved it roughly over Felix's ear. He couldn't shake the feeling that if he kept going, something horrible was going to happen, but he forced his arms to pump the plunger up and down until … *SCHLOP!* He'd sucked a purple wormy thing right out of Felix's ear.

And then Jasper knew exactly was happening.

They had been Monstered.

Felix and Jasper lay panting on the floor of the room.

Felix flicked the torchlight onto the large jar in his hand. 'Skankbamboozlers,' Felix muttered in disgust.

Two hairy, purple, worm-like monsters with horribly human faces peered out at them. They wagged their tails back and forth and laughed madly at the two boys.

'Those! *Inside* our brains – ugh!' Felix shivered.

'We should have known,' Jasper replied. 'Sore eyes, fuzzy head, confusion. Do you think we failed?'

Felix shrugged. 'We were Scrambled good.' He gave the jar a vicious shake.

'They must have got in through the headphones,' Jasper added. He knew his class teacher Stenka wouldn't let them live this down in a hurry. 'We didn't even wear our earplugs or nosepegs to block the inlets to the brain.' Jasper pulled the unused plugs and pegs from his hunt belt with a hopeless expression.

'But Sir Tavish said it was a test on Morphers!'

Skankbamboozlers

Weird human-like face

Sniggering little terror

Species: Skankbamboozler
Order: Scrambler

Felix glared at the Skankbamboozlers again. 'And what's with the lights?' he murmured as he made a shadow bunny jump across the beam of the torch.

Usually, as soon as the test was finished, the lights would come on, the door would unlock, and a voice would come over the intercom telling you to *'proceed to the exit'*. But so far ... nothing.

Felix froze, his shadow bunny caught in mid-hop. 'Unless of course, the monsters have teamed up. Like Sir Tavish was going on about.'

Felix was staring at something directly behind Jasper.

Suddenly the lights not coming on made sense. The test wasn't over.

'The Morpher – it's behind me, isn't it?' Jasper whispered.

Felix gulped.

Jasper turned around very slowly.

Four dark blue slits had appeared on the wall and were looking right at them.

'Eyes!' whispered Felix.

The walls of the room began to *breathe*. The paint turned from grey to a dark, moist red. Jasper felt the torch fall from his fingertips and hit the ground – which had turned into a soft mound of muscle.

There wasn't a monster *in* the room.

The monster *was* the room.

Jasper's body suddenly buzzed with excitement. He gritted his teeth and charged. A long rope of muscle shot towards him. It whipped around his body and snatched him up into the air. The muscle tightened around his chest. He could hardly breathe.

Felix pulled hard on Jasper's legs, trying to free him. 'What's its weakness?' he screamed desperately.

Every single monster, no matter how nasty and horrible, had a weakness. And knowing it was a monster-hunter's best weapon.

'I was hoping you'd tell me!' gasped Jasper. He racked his brain, desperately trying to think which monster could morph into a room.

The monster tightened its grip around Jasper's chest. His ribcage was being crushed. It hurt so much that his eyes welled up with tears. He hoped Felix couldn't see the fat tear he felt rolling down his cheek.

The tear splatted softly onto the floor. Suddenly, the monster-room began to shake, as if an earthquake had hit. The walls and floor of the monster-room quickly hardened, and bits of the roof began to rain down on top of

Jasper and Felix.

A strange wail came from deep inside the monster-room. The shaking stopped. There was complete silence.

Jasper's torch lay on the floor nearby, its beam shining on the Skankbamboozlers, which were cackling in their jar on the cracked floor.

The muscle binding Jasper shook once more, then broke and crumbled to dust. Jasper crashed down to the ground.

Felix and Jasper looked at each other.

Tears, Jasper thought to himself. That was one weakness he wouldn't forget in a hurry.

The lights came on, and an exit sign lit up over the door. 'Please proceed to the exit,' a voice ordered.

They didn't need to be told twice.

The hall was buzzing with excited chatter. That had *not* been a normal test. It was much harder than usual.

Jasper and Felix sat with a group of dejected-looking kids from their class.

'Stupid piece-of-rubbish Skankbamboozlers,' Felix muttered.

Rumour had it that the test was actually the pre-Hunt exam. Jasper really hoped the rumour was wrong – it was more luck than skill that had got them through the test.

The students who scored the highest on the pre-Hunt exam would be picked to go on a Hunt. A *real* Hunt, on the trail of *wild* monsters. And, of course, going on a Hunt meant going to the outside world. No teachers, no prefects – it would be just them and the monsters. Jasper was excited just thinking about it.

A bunch of surly looking prefects dressed in camouflage gear patrolled up and down the hall, handing out penalty points to anyone who gave them even the slightest excuse. The head prefect, Bruno, was keeping particularly close to Jasper's table. Bruno took great pleasure in punishing anyone he could lay his hands on, and for some reason he especially liked tormenting Jasper and his friends.

All the kids in Jasper's class wanted to go on a Hunt. But Saffy was *desperate* to go on one. She was convinced that once she was back

21

in the outside world, she'd be able to escape Monstrum House for good.

Not that she had anywhere she wanted to escape *to*. Jasper knew that Saffy wasn't interested in going home. She didn't get on very well with her parents and had been shipped around to heaps of different schools before landing at Monstrum House. But it was a matter of pride. She wanted to escape, just to prove that she *could*. Saffy had been nicknamed Houdini for being able to break out of any school. Monstrum House was the only school so far to beat her, and Saffy did *not* like being beaten.

But if the test had really been the pre-Hunt exam, then Saffy was in trouble too. It looked as though she had done just as badly as Felix and Jasper. Her test partner, Callum, had ended up in the school hospital because his foot had morphed into an apple tree. Having a partner hospitalised really didn't look good on your score sheet.

'At least he likes apples,' Saffy kept saying, almost to herself.

'QUIET!' Bruno bellowed.

The chatter in the hall dropped to a soft muttering as Stenka marched into the hall, followed by the other first-year teachers.

Stenka glared at the students until absolute silence had fallen. Jasper fought the urge to do something funny to break the silence. He knew from experience that Stenka wasn't amused by his jokes. And nothing ever seemed quite so funny after being sent to a monster-infested punishment room, or made to run the penalty course every night for a week.

'For months we have been preparing you for the pre-Hunt exam,' said Stenka slowly.

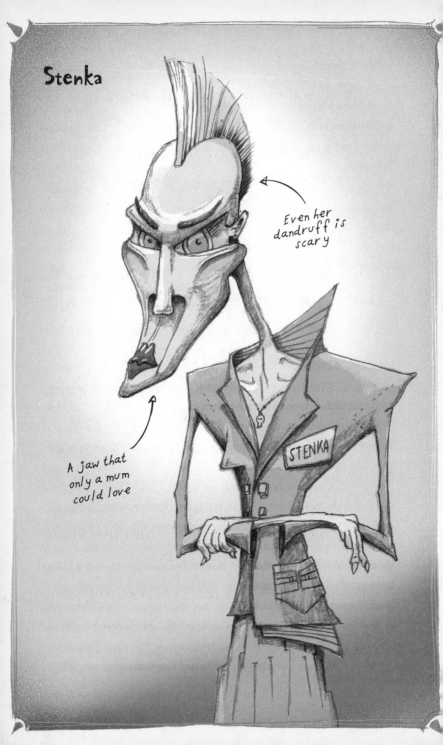

Jasper squirmed lower in his seat and dropped his gaze.

'So who can explain why all your results are so POOR?' Stenka exploded. Every student in the room jumped.

'Why didn't anyone tell us it was the exam?' one boy muttered.

Stenka turned to him, her eyes lit up like a Christmas tree. She snapped her fingers and two grinning prefects dragged the boy out of the hall. Jasper didn't want to know what the poor guy's punishment would be.

Stenka turned back to the rest of the students. 'Any other questions?' she asked sweetly, before continuing. 'We expected at least half of you to be going on your first Hunt in the coming weeks. Instead, based on your results, only two pairs demonstrated the bare minimum required.'

Felix looked sheepishly at Jasper. 'Guess we didn't make it then,' he whispered.

'SILENCE!' Stenka hissed, taking a menacing step towards Felix. Felix yelped and clamped his lips together.

Stenka's icy gaze fell on Jasper. 'Jasper McPhee, Felix Brown and Saffron Dominguez – report to my office immediately. As for the rest of you ...' She nodded to Bruno, then turned on her heel and clipped out of the hall.

Before Jasper, Felix and Saffy even had a chance to stand, Stenka's mohawk swung back around the doorway. 'I SAID IMMEDIATELY!'

Jasper, Felix and Saffy jumped to their feet and followed Stenka out of the hall. Jasper noticed the prefects smirking at them as they made their way through the doors, and Bruno wore the nastiest smirk of all.

Stenka led the way through the maze of corridors. Jasper had a pretty good sense of direction, but he had already decided that it was *impossible* to keep track of where the Monstrum House offices were.

'Last time I was sent to Stenka's office I left a trail of breadcrumbs behind me,' Saffy whispered as they trailed behind Stenka. 'When I tried to follow the crumbs back, they only led around in circles, and I ended up back at her office. She was waiting for me with a dust pan and brush.'

Stenka stopped at the door to her office. Jasper shuddered. He *hated* going into Stenka's office. Terrifying, shadowy pictures were painted on the wall, accentuated by glistening, dark red curtains. Her desk had framed pictures of half-eaten body parts on it, and a bright light was perfectly positioned so that it blinded you as you stepped inside the room.

But what really got to Jasper today was the fact that there was something that looked like a computer in the room. It had been ages since Jasper had seen a computer – and here one was, right in front of him.

Jasper, Saffy and Felix all craned their necks to try to get a better look at the screen. Jasper saw it had a map on it, with dots that moved.

It's some kind of GPS! thought Jasper.

In response, Stenka quickly tapped a key and the screen went blank.

Stenka's office

Is that ... a computer?

'Sit,' she ordered.

They sat down in the seats in front of Stenka's desk.

'Did any of you bother to study for this exam at all?' Stenka glowered, flicking through her notes. 'I expected more from you.How is it possible that out of an entire year level, only Saffron and Callum knew not to assume that there would only be one monster in the room?' Stenka stared pointedly at Jasper and Felix.

'And then to allow direct access to an inlet? You must know by now that headphones are the second most common access route for Scramblers! The only more common way to let a Scrambler into your head is by washing your face in Scrambler-infested water, but we thought *that* would be too obvious a scenario.'

It had been a mistake to use the headphones in the test room.

'We thought there might be instructions on the headphones,' Felix mumbled.

Stenka turned to Felix. 'You mean, instructions that somehow couldn't be put over the intercom in the room?' she fumed.

Felix looked away. 'Oh yeah, right.'

'And your fear-control was deplorable. I have spoken to Master Poon and arranged for you both to undergo intensive Rest and Relaxation sessions beginning tomorrow afternoon.'

Jasper groaned. Rest and Relaxation classes were by far the worst classes at Monstrum House. The students were told to relax by using fear-control exercises. Their teacher, Master Poon, spent the entire class terrifying them at the same time as yelling at them to relax. Master Poon was like some crazed superhuman army general. Jasper was *not* looking forward to extra classes.

'And Ms Dominguez,' Stenka turned towards Saffy. 'Callum will take a while to recover. They aren't called *Hobble*morphs for nothing!'

No-one said a word. Jasper waited to hear what would happen to them now. He imagined their three heads mounted on Stenka's wall like gruesome trophies.

'Still,' Stenka continued. 'The other first years' results were an utter disgrace. And of course we must consider your performance on the Task last term. But still, you had better prove yourselves in the Hunt if you want any hunt captain to choose you for their crew in the future.'

Jasper, Felix and Saffy sat up in their seats.

'You performed poorly on the test, but you just managed to score enough points to scrape a pass. And we are running low on hunt crews right now. Any more questions?'

Jasper, Felix and Saffy all shook their heads.

'Which bring us to … tags.' Stenka reached into her desk drawer and pulled out a gun.

Felix instinctively put up both his hands in surrender. 'It wasn't us! We don't have any tags!' he yelped.

Stenka stared at him, the smallest hint of a smile twitching at the corner of her mouth. 'No, Felix,' she said softly. 'You need to get tagged.'

What did she mean, *get tagged?*

'It's a simple process,' continued Stenka. 'We just insert a tag into your neck and then we can keep track of where you are. It's extremely painful, but we find it a very reliable way to trace our hunt crews. Now, who's first?'

Stenka came closer with the gun. 'You first, Mr Brown. Come here.'

Trembling, Felix went over to Stenka's desk.

'Stop shaking!' Stenka said, and clicked the gun, loading a tag in readiness. She held it against the back of Felix's neck. 'If the tag doesn't go in exactly the right spot, it could cause some damage. You have to stand perfectly still.' Then she paused. 'Now, I do have to inform you that if you don't want to be tagged, that is completely up to you,' she said sweetly.

The tagging gun

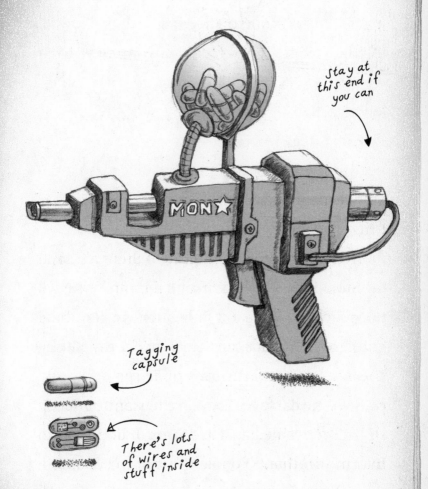

Stay at this end if you can

Tagging capsule

There's lots of wires and stuff inside

'But you can't go on a Hunt without a tag.'

Felix's eyes were darting all over the place.

'It's all for your own good,' Stenka tutted. 'If you become separated from your crew, then we need some way of finding you. Or what's left of you.'

Felix's legs wobbled.

'But if you don't want to be tagged, just say the word.'

Felix fainted.

Stenka stared at the gun. 'I haven't even tagged him yet. But given he didn't say no …' She reached down and pulled the trigger of the gun. There was a sharp crack as Stenka shot a small capsule into the back of Felix's neck.

Felix woke up with a yell, then fainted again.

'Unbelievable. And to think he really is a Brown Brother.' Stenka shook her head in disgust as she wrenched Felix out of the way.

Felix came from a family of monster-hunters. His brothers had a reputation as some of the best and bravest monster-hunters to come out of Monstrum House. But Felix didn't always seem to follow in their footsteps.

'Saffron,' Stenka ordered. 'Stand here. Completely still.'

Saffy stood up and walked to the desk. 'Haven't you ever heard of a tracking bracelet?' she growled.

Saffy's jaw clenched, but she didn't even cry out as the tag was inserted into her neck.

'Yes,' Stenka replied as she lovingly reloaded the gun, 'but you can take *those* off. Now, Mr McPhee ...'

Jasper noticed Stenka's computer screen had come back to life, and two flashing dots had appeared. *Those dots must be signals from Saffy's and Felix's tags*, thought Jasper.

Jasper looked at the others. It looked like all the blood had been drained from their faces. Felix was still out cold.

'Oh, for goodness' sake,' muttered Stenka, putting down the gun. Then she did something Jasper never thought Stenka would do. She reached into her desk drawer and pulled out some chocolate. 'Eat,' she said to Saffy. 'You will need the sugar hit if you want to walk any further than my office door.'

Felix woke up at the mention of sugar, and dragged himself to the table. 'Why didn't you say so?' he said, shoving a big piece of chocolate into his mouth. 'This almost makes it worthwhile!'

'Hardly,' said Saffy, scowling, as she ate her chocolate. But the way the scowl fell from her face reminded Jasper of just how good chocolate could be.

'Come on, then,' said Jasper.

He tried not to move a muscle as Stenka loaded the gun again.

'I should just say that tagging brings with it the possibility of some … side-effects,' Stenka hissed into his ear.

Then there was a sharp crack, and the air around him seemed to shatter.

'You're done,' Jasper heard Stenka say, but her voice sounded a long way away. It felt as though he had just been whacked on the back of his neck with a hammer. A burning sensation started to spread up his neck and along his shoulders. He could make out three dots flashing on the computer screen in front of him, before everything went black.

Then the whispering started. The spooky, strange whispering that no-one else could hear.

Kom …

Jasper tried to open his eyes, but it was as

though they were cemented shut. He wanted the whispering to stop, but the harder he tried to block it out, the louder it became.

Hyrem klepspar ... Jasp ...

Jasper put his hands over his ears. He could feel a cry growing up from deep inside his chest. *What do you want? Leave me alone!* Jasper screamed inside his head.

NAO JASP ... KOM NAO.

There was another crack and Jasper felt his cheek begin to burn. His eyes snapped open. Stenka stood in front of him, her hand raised. Saffy and Felix both had their mouths hanging open in astonishment.

Jasper put a hand gingerly to his cheek, and he realised that Stenka had just slapped him.

Stenka frogmarched Jasper out of her office.

'Walk,' she commanded. She steered him around the corridors until they were standing in front of a black door.

Stenka passed her beady black eyes over Jasper. 'I had hoped you weren't so far into the first stage. But a reaction like that to tagging can only mean that you are more affected than we thought. You have had more exposure to wild monsters than most first-year students. Let's just hope it isn't too late,' she said.

Jasper had no idea what she was talking about, but he didn't like the sound of it. 'It's not too late. Really, I –'

'Well,' Stenka cut him off, 'there's only one way for us to find out.'

Stenka turned the door handle. It was inky black inside the room. 'I'll be back to check on you,' she said, and pushed Jasper inside.

41

The room was dark. Jasper heard the wind howl outside, whipping snow against the window panes. Inside, the room was deathly still. Anyone would think it was empty. But Jasper knew there were no empty rooms at Monstrum House.

Jasper waited for the cold chill to run down his spine, the signal that a monster was there, about to attack. But there was no cold chill. *Strange*, he thought. *There mustn't be a monster.* Jasper sighed in relief. *I'm safe! But if there's no monster, what's in this room? Why did Stenka bring me here?*

He didn't have to wonder for long. His elbow was clamped tightly and he was pulled off his feet. Jasper tried to hit out at whatever had him, but his arm was pulled painfully behind his back.

'One more move and the bone will snap,' a soft voice warned.

'OK! OK!'

'No,' the voice replied. 'It's not OK. You assumed you were safe. And you weren't.'

Jasper's arm was jerked back again, and he winced in pain. 'OK, I'll never assume anything again,' he moaned. The voice chuckled softly, and then his arm was released.

Jasper slumped onto the floor, and waited for the pain in his shoulder to let up. The lights in the room came on. Jasper took a deep breath and turned around.

A small, thin man with a curly handlebar moustache sat cross-legged on the floor. He was nibbling at a peanut butter and jam sandwich.

'Señor Hermes,' the man introduced himself, holding out his hand for Jasper to shake.

'Um. Jasper. Jasper McPhee.' Jasper leant forward and shook the man's hand. The moment they shook hands Señor Hermes had Jasper pinned down flat on his stomach, his arm twisted behind his back again.

'I see you are a slow learner,' Señor Hermes sighed. 'What was the first thing I said?'

'Um. *One more move and the bone will snap,*' Jasper replied.

'No, no. After that. The bit about never assuming.'

Jasper's muscles felt as though they were being torn from his body. 'Never assume I'm safe. Got it,' he wheezed.

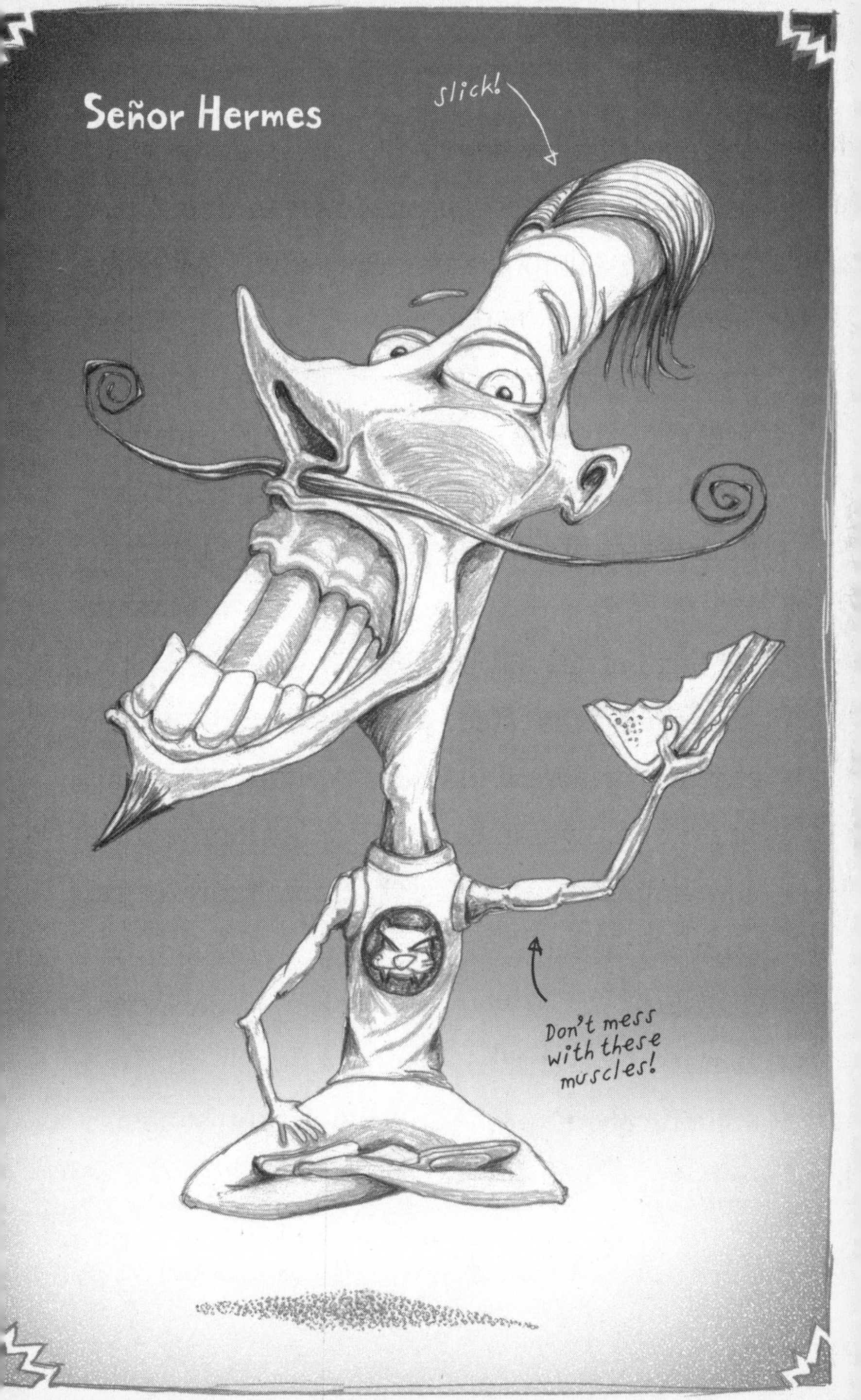
Señor Hermes
slick!
Don't mess with these muscles!

'Are you sure? Because I can hold your arm longer if you need some more time to think.' Señor Hermes took another bite of his sandwich and waited for Jasper to nod, before releasing his arm.

'OK,' said Hermes. 'Now sit.'

Jasper stepped backwards until he was sure he had left enough space between him and Hermes. He squatted down, ready to jump at the slightest movement.

Hermes chuckled. 'No, really. Sit. Cross-legged. And close your eyes.' Jasper shook his head.

'Never assume I'm safe,' Jasper replied. 'I'm not that stupid.'

Señor Hermes looked Jasper in the eyes. 'That is the first rule,' he said seriously. 'But the second rule in my class is that you must do as I tell you.'

Your class? Jasper thought.

'Yes, this is a private class. Now close your eyes.'

Jasper's arm was still aching. He rubbed his shoulder and sighed. He sat down in front of Hermes, and closed his eyes.

He felt Señor Hermes' fingers brush across his eyelids. Jasper began to shake. He couldn't help it. His whole body was shaking as though he had been shoved into a freezer.

'The whispering will come,' Señor Hermes explained quietly. 'It will come, and you will control it. You have a strong brain, but it needs to be taught how to understand the whispering.'

Jasper opened his eyes. 'Hang on. The whispering? You can hear the whispering too?'

Hermes cocked his head to one side. 'I'm sorry, Jasper. Most of my students are older than you. I can see I am going too quickly.

Whispering doesn't usually develop until students are at least in their second year and have a better understanding of monsters. Let me explain a little before we begin. Yes, I can hear the whispering, but I can't hear what you can. I can hear whispering of my own. All the Whispered can. There are quite a few of us, you know.'

Jasper's jaw fell open. 'The Whispered?'

'That's the name for people who have been bitten by a monster,' Hermes said simply. 'Like you.'

Jasper couldn't believe what he was hearing. 'I haven't been bitten by a monster! I mean I've been Monstered here at school but –'

'No, no. A monster bite is different,' said Señor Hermes. 'You were bitten by a Scrambler, species Vernonvex, I believe. It happened when you were a small child.'

'But … what?' asked Jasper. He'd never felt more confused.

Señor Hermes looked at Jasper and sighed. 'Let me start from the beginning,' he said, settling into his seat. 'You see, monsters are full of monsterness.'

'*Monsterness*?'

'Yes. Monsterness is what makes a monster a monster. When monsters hatch, they are like relatively normal creatures. They might look like a spider, for example, or an octopus. But monsterness causes them to mutate and form monster characteristics.'

'OK,' said Jasper, trying not to look surprised to hear that monsters *hatched*. Right now, there were more important things to find out. 'But what has this got to do with the whispering?'

'Ah, well, the thing about monsterness is that it can be *transferred*,' said Hermes.

Jasper didn't like the sound of that.

'You see, when a monster bites someone,' Hermes continued, 'some of this monsterness

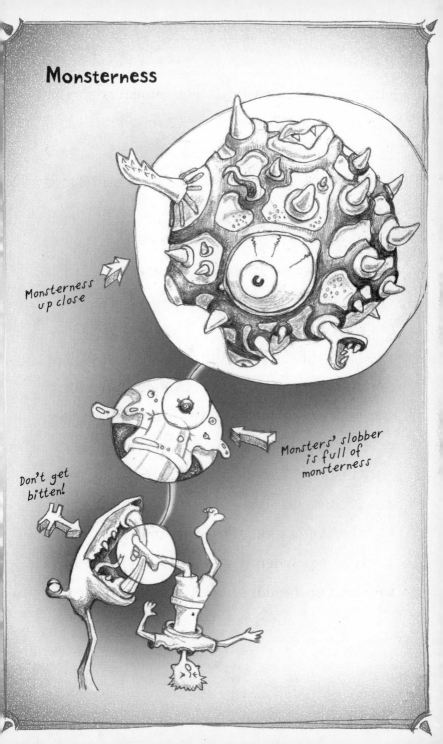

is *transferred* to its victim. A bit like the way germs might be transferred from an animal bite. You are *infected*, in a way. It's a very slow process, but the whispering you hear is essentially the start of ... How can I put this? ... It's the start of you becoming a monster.'

'I am be-be-becoming a monster?' Jasper stuttered.

'Precisely!' said Señor Hermes. 'And you have started to hear the whispering because your monsterness is excited by the environment here at Monstrum House. Anywhere cold, dark and scary will cause it to grow inside you. Any negative experience – such as the painful tagging you just had – will make it stronger.'

'I am a *monster*?' asked Jasper again.

'Well, a part-monster at most, I should think,' said Hermes. 'But it's not all bad – it can even be used to your advantage. Whispering is the first monster characteristic to develop. It is like an antenna into the monster world. For a monster-hunter, that can be an invaluable tool.'

Jasper shook his head. He didn't really get how it could be an 'invaluable tool'. He felt like he was hyperventilating. He wished he had Felix's asthma puffer with him. 'Wolfman, I'm like Wolfman,' he mumbled, 'or a vampire, or a ... a ...'

'Keep calm,' said Hermes. 'Let me finish, and then you can decide whether you need to panic.'

'Need to panic?! Are you mad? You just said I'm becoming a MONSTER!'

Jasper was feeling giddy. He didn't want to become a monster. Surely the teachers would have some medicine, some antidote?

'I'm sorry, Jasper. This isn't a mistake and there isn't any antidote.' Hermes looked Jasper in the eye. 'The harder you try to block out the whispering, the louder it becomes, yes?'

Jasper nodded.

'What you hear is the voice of the monster you *could* become. It's not a real monster. It's your own monster side trying to speak to you and guide you into the path of monsters. It's a whisper now, but ignoring it will make it shout to be heard.'

He paused. 'You already feel excited when you are around monsters, don't you?'

'I feel a kind of ... buzz,' said Jasper. 'I get excited. Something clicks. One minute I'm scared and the next, I kind of just know what to do.'

'You see – that is your monster side becoming excited. But you can *use* that on a Hunt!'

Jasper was shocked. If the reason he got a buzz hunting monsters was because his monster side was developing, was it really a good idea to be going on a Hunt?

Señor Hermes continued. 'Left untreated, you will gain more monster characteristics and, eventually, become more monster than human. But if you learn how to *understand* the whispering, you can use it. I will guide you through the principles of doing so.'

'Now, when the whispering comes,' said Señor Hermes calmly, 'I want you to see the words you hear in your mind. Then I want you to look at each word carefully, and try to make sense of it.'

Jasper felt uncertain, but he closed his eyes and let Señor Hermes' fingers brush over his eyelids again. The whispering rose up inside his body. It was strong, and kept getting louder.

JAAA ... SPEER! NAAOO. KOOMM FREEE ...

'What is it saying?' Hermes' voice broke through the whispering, and a blank piece of paper appeared in Jasper's mind.

JAAA ... SPEEEER!

The word formed on the page in front of Jasper. The letters were spooky and ancient-looking, but he recognised the word straight away.

'My name! It's my name!'

'Good, next word!'

NAAAOOO.

The letters appeared again.

Naaaooo. Naao. Nao. Each of the words Jasper tried was crossed out on the page. He looked at them again. *Now.*

'Now? I think it says now!'

'Keep going, Jasper!' said Hermes.

KOOOOMMM FREEE.

Koom. Kom. Com. The words were crossed out. *Come?*

'I think it's come. Come free.'

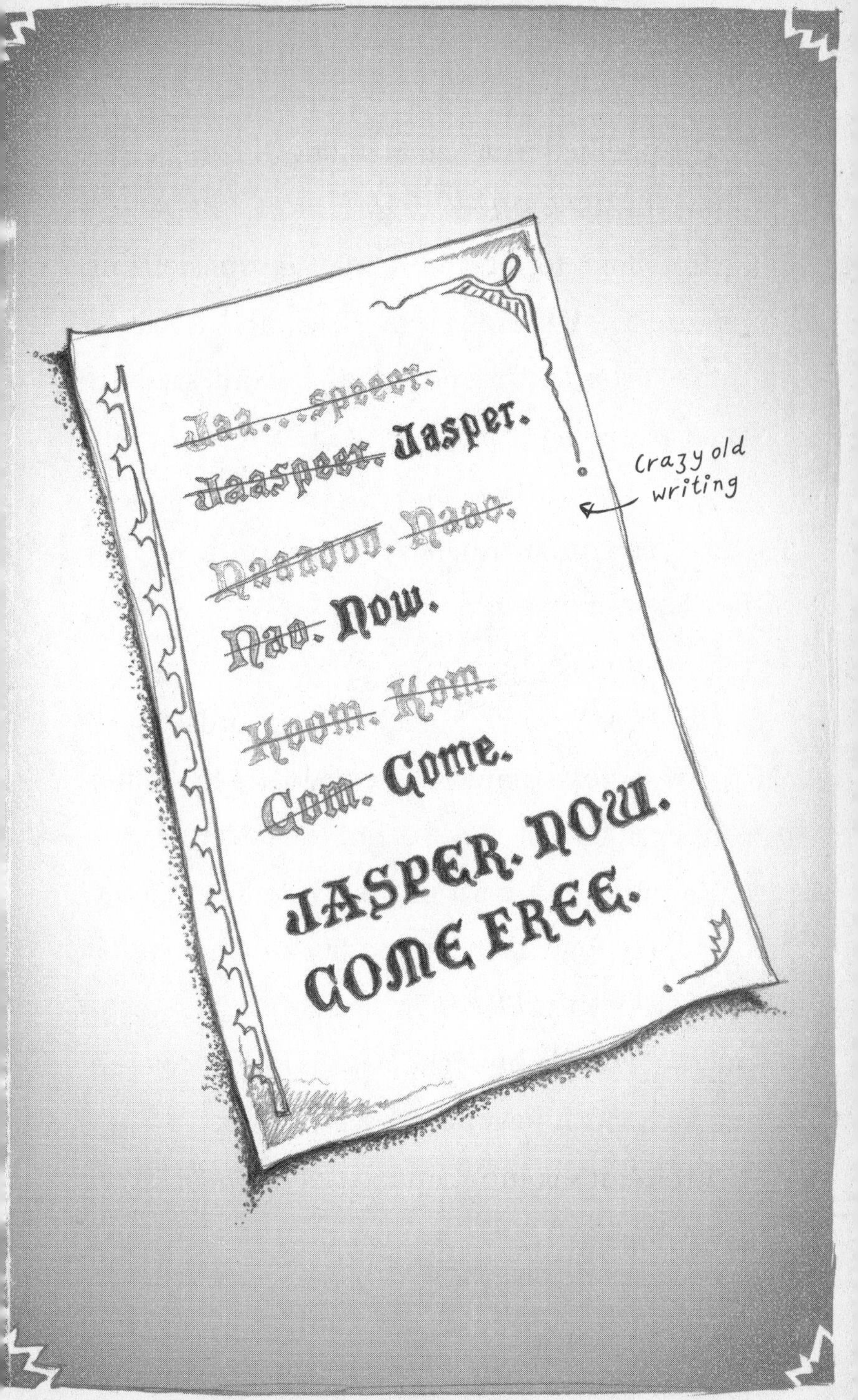
Jaa...speer.
Jaaspeer. Jasper.
Naaaoon. Naae.
Nao. Now.
Koom. Kom.
Com. Come.
JASPER. NOW.
COME FREE.
Crazy old writing

The finished words lined up neatly in Jasper's mind: 'JASPER. NOW. COME FREE,' he read.

'It wants to be free,' said Hermes. 'Now control it. Tell it no!'

'No!' shouted Jasper. And the inky words faded away on the page, until there was nothing left.

Jasper couldn't believe it. The whispering had listened to *him!*

When Jasper opened his eyes, he saw Señor Hermes sipping at a mug of hot chocolate. 'It took you a while, but with practice it will get easier. Soon you will have the ability to understand the words within seconds.' He popped a marsh-mallow into his hot chocolate. 'Hot chocolate?' he asked, pushing a mug towards Jasper.

Jasper drank it in one go. Neither of them

said anything for a while.

'Was that some sort of mind reading?' Jasper asked finally. 'I mean, because I was reading stuff in my mind.'

'In a way,' said Señor Hermes. 'But you were only reading the words you already hear, in your own mind. You are learning to understand your monster side.'

My monster side. Oh yeah. Jasper sighed.

'Having a monster side does not make you a monster. The monsterness does not have a body, or a form. It is simply the essence of a monster. Little more than a voice at this point.' Señor Hermes looked at Jasper and smiled. 'You are far from alone, you know. Many people have quite advanced monsterness, and still control it successfully. Why else do you think the teachers here are so scary?' he winked.

Jasper nearly choked on his marshmallows.

'You mean – the teachers have *all* been bitten?'

'Yes, we have. I am sure you've noticed that Mr Golag, like most monsters, can't stand bright lights, Von Strasser is slightly Scrambled, and Stenka loves nothing more than to frighten people,' he said. 'But we all have complete control of our monster side.'

Jasper looked closely at Hermes. He didn't *seem* very monster-like.

There was a sharp rap on the door and Stenka marched into the room. 'Sorry to interrupt your cosy chat,' she sneered. 'What is your opinion, Hermes? Do you think it is too late?'

Jasper thought he could detect a note of hope in her voice.

'I don't think so,' said Hermes. 'There are no monster characteristics other than whispering at this stage.'

'Very well,' said Stenka. 'He will do.' She

yanked Jasper out of the room and marched him through the maze of corridors.

'I have told the others your strange behaviour was a side-effect of being tagged,' said Stenka when they reached the doors to her office. 'They believe you have been to see the nurse. We are going to keep it that way. Understood?'

Jasper nodded. He wasn't sure he wanted to tell Saffy and Felix about the whole 'being a monster' thing, anyway. They were his friends, but maybe this would change things. They were supposed to be monster-*hunters*, not *monsters*.

Jasper still had a thousand questions on his mind.

'Questions will have to wait,' said Stenka. 'Because now it is time to Hunt.'

Stenka swiftly led Jasper, Felix and Saffy out of her office and down the hallway.

'Are you OK?' Felix whispered to Jasper as soon as Stenka was far enough ahead. 'You were gone for, like, two hours. We had to wait in Stenka's freaky office the whole time!'

'It's a long story,' Jasper mumbled.

'That was a cracker of a slap,' said Saffy.

Jasper grimaced. 'Tell me about it, my jaw is still aching.'

'Well, to be fair, you were lying on the

ground, twitching and squeaking like a guinea pig,' Saffy smiled. 'I was about to pour cold water on your head, but the slap worked.'

Jasper hoped she was joking. He'd heard the whispering ever since he started at Monstrum House, but he'd never had a fit like that.

Stenka turned on her heel. 'Enough chitter chatter. Get a move on.'

Jasper saluted Stenka behind her back.

'I saw that, Mr McPhee. Don't think getting accepted to go on a Hunt will get you out of trouble,' she growled.

Jasper sighed. He hated the way the teachers seemed to tap into his thoughts. He wondered how they did it. Were his thoughts being written down on a piece of paper in Stenka's head?

Finally, Stenka stopped short. 'Here we are,' she said. They were at the bottom of a dark staircase.

'Are you sure this is safe?' Felix asked.

Jasper could see what Felix meant. There were big holes in the stairs where it looked like some poor kids had fallen through the rotting wood, and the banister was just a flimsy piece of twine threaded through hooks. Two carved stone monsters guarded the base of the stairs.

'It doesn't look like it goes anywhere,' Saffy commented. Light shone through a window at the top of the staircase.

Stenka ignored her. She pressed the eye of one of the stone monsters, and a door appeared at the top of the rickety stairs where the window had been.

Stenka began to climb the stairs. 'Well? Are you coming?' she asked. 'This is it. Hunt Headquarters.'

At the top of the stairs, she turned to them. 'Before you go through, I just need to tell you

Staircase to nowhere

Press on this eyeball

After you!

that where I am taking you is top-secret,' said Stenka. 'The very best of the best. Extremely high-tech. We have spared no expense getting this right. The Secret Service has nothing compared to what we have here.'

Jasper could feel the excitement bubbling up inside him.

'Congratulations,' Stenka said, 'You are about to become monster-hunters. Are you ready?' Stenka was beginning to sound like a game show host, but even Felix was nodding enthusiastically.

Stenka smiled and opened the door.

The room was buzzing with activity. Tables and chairs were scattered about, and older students were frantically poring over papers.

The whole place was a complete mess. There

were piles of useless junk everywhere. Jasper tripped over a stack of dirty plates, got his feet tangled in some wire, trod on a tube of paint and kicked over a pile of papers.

'This is it?' asked Felix, less than impressed.

'I guess so ...' Jasper shrugged. Maybe there was another room? He couldn't see anything that looked high-tech. 'Although, none of the thug brigade are here,' he added as he realised that there were no prefects around.

'I knew it,' muttered Saffy. '*No expense* is right.'

A sinister grin formed on Stenka's face. 'I can't believe students always fall for that one. So predictable!' she sighed, enjoying their dismay. 'Now, down to business. Mr Mackenzie!' she turned and barked loudly.

A stressed-looking third-year boy in a red hoodie crawled out from under a table. Jasper grinned. They knew Mac – he had helped them out in the past. His hoodie had the *Hunt Captain* emblem. *Awesome*, thought Jasper. *This is actually happening.*

'Yo,' Mac called back, as he jogged over.

Stenka raised her eyebrows. 'Yo?'

'Oh, ah, I mean, how can I possibly be of assistance?' Mac smiled innocently.

'You asked for a crew. Here you go,' she said, and turned to walk away.

Mac looked at Jasper, Felix and Saffy. Jasper noticed that the panicked look on Mac's face only got worse.

'Wait!' Mac called to Stenka.

She turned innocently. 'Problem?'

'They're all Firsties!' said Mac, pointing at Jasper and the others.

'Hey!' said Saffy defensively. 'We all passed the exam.'

Mac turned to her with a look of exaggerated astonishment on his face. 'Well then, you *must* be good,' he replied.

Felix frowned. 'I think he's being sarcastic.'

'It's them or no-one,' replied Stenka, and turned on her heel.

Mac muttered a string of obscenities under his breath as he glared at Jasper, Felix and Saffy.

'Right then. I guess you're in. This is where we do the initial preparation for the Hunt. Teachers come and go if needed, but mostly it's just us. The workstation is over here,' said Mac, nodding towards a desk overflowing with junk.

'And I thought I was messy,' Felix mumbled, tossing a bicycle tyre off a chair.

Jasper sifted through the debris. 'What's all this for?'

'Functional Fixedness,' Mac replied. 'You

Inside Hunt Headquarters

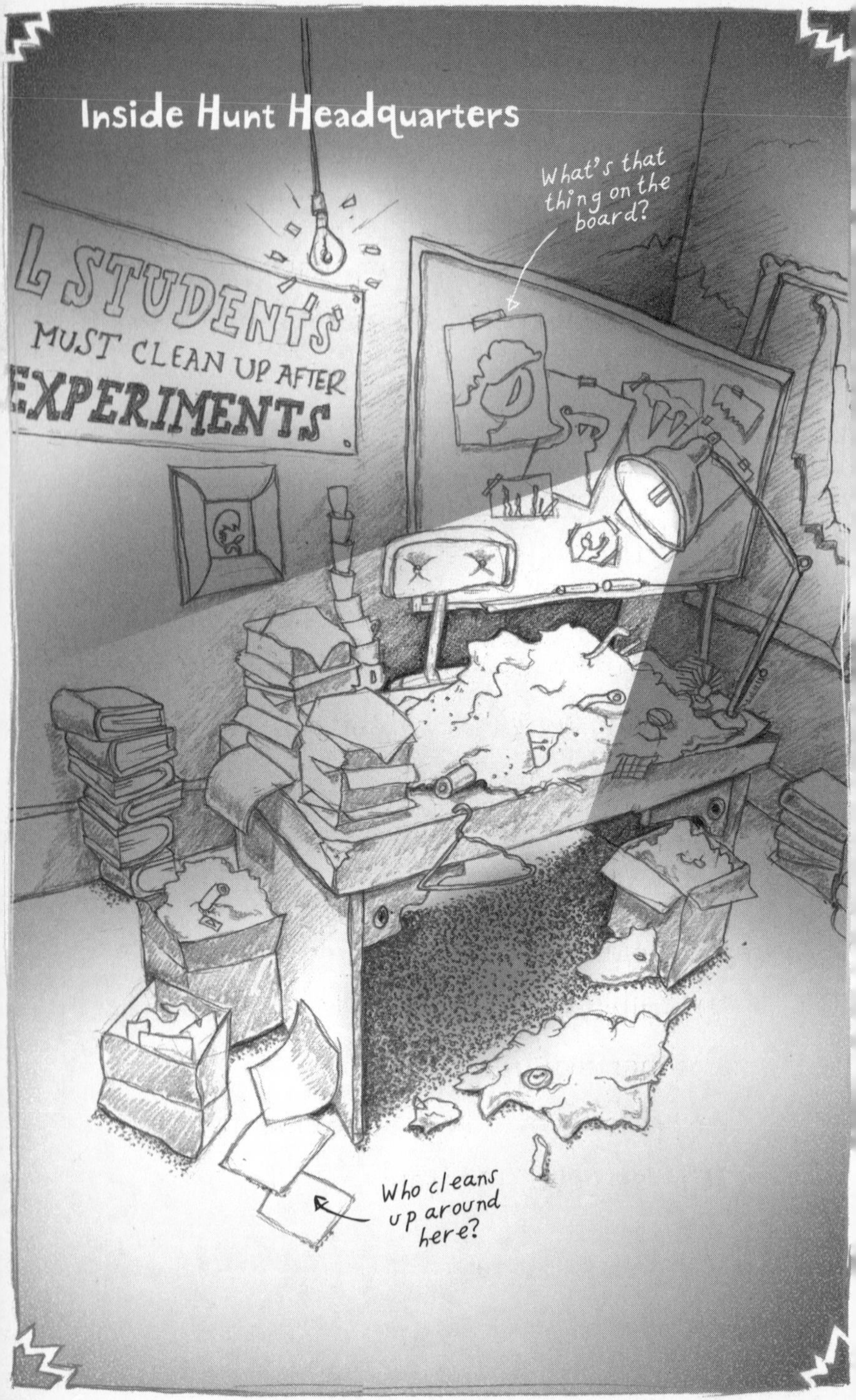

start that class in second year. Basically it's the Monstrum House version of making gadgets. You choose the junk, and make your own gadget to catch the monster. Cool, huh?' Mac nodded enthusiastically as he held up a broken coathanger.

Jasper looked at Mac. 'Cool is a monster zapper fired from your sneakers. *That* is a coat hanger. Not cool.'

'Just you wait. This baby could make a wicked monster zapper,' Mac said. He started fiddling bits of junk together.

'And what's with the picture of mud? Don't tell me – it's cool?' Felix scoffed, pulling a picture off the whiteboard.

'Definitely not cool,' Mac replied. 'And not mud either. See that green dot?'

Jasper leant over Felix's shoulder to look.

'That's its eye,' Mac said.

Saffy grabbed the photo from Felix and examined it closely. 'This is it? This is the monster?'

Mac nodded. 'Ladies and gentlemen,' he boomed theatrically, 'I have the pleasure today of introducing you to – drum roll, please – the Glibberhowl. Also known as *your worst nightmare.*'

Mac pulled a piece of paper out of his pocket and laid it on the table.

HUNT ASSIGNMENT: Lake of Terror

MONSTER ORDER: Screecher

MONSTER SPECIES: Glibberhowl

MONSTER WEAKNESS: Flame in the left nasal cavity

HABITAT: Marine

HUNT CAPTAIN: Eugene Mackenzie

DEPARTURE TIME: Tuesday 2.49pm

'Eugene?' Saffy snorted.

Mac narrowed his eyes.

'Hang on.' Jasper looked at Mac. 'A marine monster? As in, lives in the water? How are we meant to get fire up its nose if it's underwater?'

Mac gestured to the piles of junk scattered around the workstation. 'You're just going to have to start inventing,' he said.

'But we haven't even studied Functional Fixedness yet!' complained Saffy.

Mac pushed a book towards her. *'The Functional Fixedness Helpful Hints Handbook,'* Saffy read aloud.

'Knock yourself out,' said Mac.

'At least it's a Screecher and not a Muncher,' said Felix, flicking absent-mindedly through the paper spread around the workstation.

'Well, people have died of fright before,'

Mac warned. 'And there has only been one successful Glibberhowl Hunt in the whole history of Monstrum House. That was only after they drained the lake. And they only did *that* after the monster-hunters were … well, dead.'

Felix groaned. 'Why did you have to tell us that?'

'Try not to think about it,' Mac said. 'Just remember, the bigger the fright, the happier Screechers are, and the stronger they get. And a Glibberhowl is even worse. The bigger the fright, the bigger it grows. So whatever you do, *don't let it frighten you.*'

Jasper glanced at Felix, who was chewing nervously on his fingernails. *That's easier said than done*, he thought.

'OK. Last thing.' Mac swept the pile of paper off the desk. 'The lake.' He slapped a map down in front of them.

Jasper leant over the map. All the place names had been blacked out.

'Why is the destination such a mystery?' Saffy asked.

Mac looked at her seriously. 'It's a precaution. When you're on a Hunt, it's easy for monsters to get inside your head. Some Scramblers can read your thoughts like a newspaper. If you knew everything – like where Monstrum House is and where the Hunt is – how long do you think it'd take a monster to find you if the Hunt went wrong? The whole school would be in danger.'

Saffy gulped. 'So that's why, when we first came to Monstrum House, they put us into a deep sleep on the plane?'

Mac nodded. 'It's one of the reasons the teachers can't come on the Hunts with us. They know too much.'

But Jasper was still thinking about what Mac had said earlier. *Some Scramblers can read your thoughts like a newspaper ...*

'So this is where the Glibberhowl lives?' Felix asked, pointing to the map.

Mac nodded. 'And this is where we will have to go to hunt it. During the day it's a popular swimming spot, which is why it has become the perfect stalking ground for the Glibberhowl.'

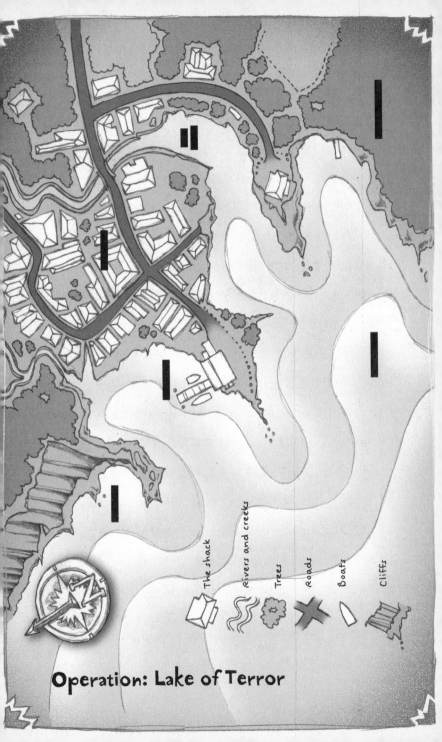

The shack

Rivers and creeks

Trees

Roads

Boats

Cliffs

Operation: Lake of Terror

Jasper thought of the lake where he used to spend holidays as a kid. He loved swimming, but there were parts of it he never went near. He always imagined the horrible things that lived way down in the dark where the sunlight couldn't reach. It felt even worse to know now that he'd probably been right.

'Glibberhowls are pretty rare, so we don't know much about them,' Mac continued quietly. 'But we do know that the Glibberhowl lies in wait at the bottom of the lake. Waiting for some poor person to swim out too deep, or get stuck by themselves. And then it strikes. We're not sure exactly *how* it attacks, because the only people who would be able to tell us are too scared to talk about it, or … dead. But we have to assume it somehow sucks you underwater.'

Saffy was beginning to squirm in her seat.

'We also know that it especially likes stalking

swimmers at dusk,' Mac went on, 'which is when we will be going in. I take it you can all swim well?'

Jasper and Felix both nodded.

Saffy looked away. 'Well,' she mumbled. 'Technically, I can swim. But actually ...'

Jasper couldn't believe it. He also couldn't help rubbing it in, even though he knew he'd probably regret it later. 'You mean little Miss Perfect, Kickboxing Champion, Best Escape Artist in the World, Speaks a Million Languages, Good at Everything, Saffron Dominguez can't *swim*?' he asked, huge grin spread across his face.

Saffy looked at him and sighed. 'I really hoped I wouldn't have to do this,' she said, then sent Jasper flying across the room with a sharp kick to his thigh.

Jasper crashed into a nearby table, upending

a model that another crew had been huddled around. 'Hey!' they yelled angrily.

Jasper apologised and meekly walked back to the workstation.

'Rub my nose in it again and I won't be aiming for your thigh,' Saffy threatened.

Mac just shook his head. 'Firsties,' he muttered and turned to Saffy. 'So, how did you get accepted to Monstrum House without being able to swim?'

Saffy grinned. 'My school records said I was an exceptional swimmer,' she replied. 'I guess Monstrum House didn't check.'

'However,' a cold voice announced from behind them, 'you can expect an intensive regime of swimming lessons when you have finished this Hunt. We have no use for hunters who can't be relied upon.'

Jasper turned to see Stenka standing behind

them, glaring at Saffy with her arms crossed.

'Thanks, *Eugene*, for bringing that to everyone's attention,' muttered Saffy.

Jasper imagined Saffy being thrown into a monster-infested pool and ordered to get out. By the look on Saffy's face, she was imagining something similar.

'And I will expect you to show us something on this Hunt,' Stenka glowered. 'Prove yourself. Student reviews have not started yet. Spring any more surprises like this on us, and you may not be offered the option of returning to Monstrum House next year.'

Saffy's face turned steely. She was about to reply when a voice boomed over the intercom: 'Crew 4 to Dock C. Transport ready to depart.'

Mac looked at his watch. 'Already? OK, we'll go over the rest when we get there. Let's go.'

'What, now?' Felix asked.

'That's what the assignment said. *Tuesday 2.49pm* – or didn't you read that bit?' Mac sounded slightly annoyed.

'Yeah, but I thought they meant Tuesday 2.49pm next week or month, or something,' Felix mumbled.

Jasper had been thinking the same thing. How were they supposed to go straight into a Hunt?

'That's what your school lessons are for,' Stenka replied. 'What do you think we've been teaching you? You need to be able to respond to Hunt calls as soon as the Surveillance Units inform us of monster activity.'

'We'd better hurry. It's a quarter to,' said Mac.

'Enjoy,' Stenka said. 'And stay alert. You are all new at this, so *listen* to Mac, and use *whatever* knowledge you have. I will be keeping track of you.'

Jasper didn't like the fact that Stenka was staring directly at him. Suddenly he was frightened. What if he heard the whispering? What if he couldn't control it? He might put everyone in danger.

He wasn't ready. He didn't want to go on a Hunt. Not yet. 'What about my, um, medicine?' he asked Stenka quietly.

'You will just have to make do with what the *nurse* gave you already,' said Stenka.

'Let's go.' Mac had shoved all the papers and junk from their workstation into a few large backpacks. Everyone hoisted a bag onto their backs. 'Wish us luck!' Mac called to Stenka as he jogged from the room with Jasper, Felix and Saffy in tow.

'You'll need it,' Stenka said grimly.

Mac didn't slow down. They ran through the hallways of Monstrum House until Mac stopped in front of an old rotting wooden door. He ripped back an ivy plant that was growing over it to reveal a sign:

DOCK C

Jasper had never heard of the docks before. It was like the school kept sprouting new parts.

'Transport departing in thirty seconds,' came

a monotone voice over the intercom.

'Quick!' Mac ordered. 'The transport is on auto-pilot. It won't hang around.' He wrenched open the door to Dock C.

Behind the door, a muddy old military truck rumbled in a garage. A large canopy was open in the back of the truck.

'That's how we're getting there?' Saffy groaned. 'This school seriously sucks.'

Mac chucked his backpack into the back of the truck and jumped on board. The others threw their bags up. Felix and Saffy had just clambered in when the garage door swung open automatically.

'Jump on!' Mac cried.

'Jasper!' Felix yelled as Jasper slipped in the mud.

The truck took off out the garage door.

Jasper sprang up from the mud and sprinted

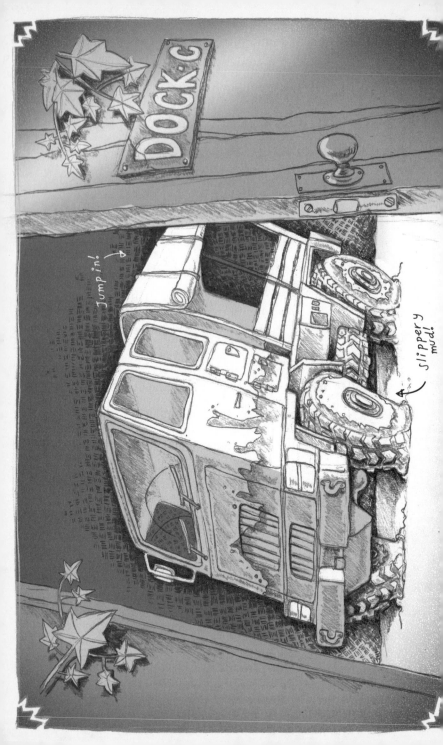

towards the truck. He might have been worried about the Hunt, but he still didn't want to get left behind at school. He'd *never* live that down.

Mac and Felix stretched their arms out. Jasper just managed to grab hold of Mac's hand. Saffy grabbed him by his hoodie and hoisted him into the truck as it swerved around a corner.

'Firsties,' Mac sighed again and closed the canopy.

It was dark in the truck, though some sunlight peeked through the cracks in the canopy. Jasper hoped it wouldn't be a long trip. They had only been driving for twenty minutes, and already he was bored.

The truck was empty except for some old cardboard boxes, a few fishing nets and a large pile of oily rags.

'OK, well, night-night,' Mac yawned and settled down, using one of the backpacks as a pillow.

'It's three in the afternoon!' Saffy remarked.

Mac opened an eye. 'It won't be soon. And the more sleep you get now, the better. Trust me. Anyway, the music will start soon.'

'Hang on, you mean like the music on the plane when we first came to Monstrum House?' Felix asked. 'I hated that music.'

Soft music began to play over the speakers in the back of the truck.

Mac smiled.'Exactly,' he said.

'Can't we – ahhhhh –' Felix yawned and rubbed his eyes. 'Turn it … turn it *offffffzzzzz.*' Felix's head dropped to his chest and he started to snore.

Saffy had quietly nodded off too. Jasper tried to keep his eyes open – he peered through the cracks in the canopy, trying to see where they were going. But it was hopeless. He lay down against his backpack and instantly fell asleep.

Jasper woke up with a start. He blinked his eyes and rubbed them. *I must be dreaming*, he thought.

'No way,' Felix murmured behind Jasper.

'Is this for real?' Saffy joined in.

'I dunno. Pinch me.' Jasper immediately regretted the invitation. 'OK, that hurt. So I'm not dreaming.'

'This is soooooo awesome,' Felix grinned.

They weren't in the truck anymore. Instead, they were in the coolest apartment Jasper had ever seen.

The lounge room was full of stuff Jasper had forgotten even existed: a huge television screen

took up most of one wall, and there were computer games, DVDs and a whole bookshelf full of games, cards, comic books, scrapbooks and pencils. Jasper was itching to grab a pencil and start sketching.

His eyes wandered over to a huge desk set out with paper, pens and a range of textbooks. Jasper flicked through *The Massive Manuscript of Monstering Mechanics*, before he spotted *Sub-Monster Species and Surrounds*. He looked over his shoulder, but the others were checking out what else was in the room. He quickly flicked to the Scrambler section.

Vernonvex. He stopped his finger under the name and quickly read the opening excerpt.

The Vernonvex species of Scrambler is one of the most cunning in its order. The Vernonvex preys on shy, young individuals, and will often spend days stalking the victim before striking. Its intent is to confuse and frustrate the victim.

Although solid, it has a wispy, smoke-like appearance and accesses the brain through the victim's nostrils. The Vernonvex is often a cause of hayfever.

'No way!' Felix exclaimed again as he opened a fridge full of soft drinks and chocolate bars.

Jasper slammed the book shut.

'It's like we're in one of those really fancy hotel rooms that movie stars stay in,' Felix said. He took a slurp from a can and then shoved an entire chocolate bar into his mouth.

'Welcome to the Hunt!' The door to the room swung open. Mac wheeled a shopping trolley full of take-away food boxes into the room.

'Hamburger and chips!' Saffy cried, helping Mac unpack.

'One Hawaiian pizza, one supreme pizza, one bowl of wedges, two strawberry milkshakes, two chocolate milkshakes, four chocolate sundaes, a spaghetti bolognese, a sushi platter, hamburgers with the lot, chips, a Greek salad, a fruit salad, and tomorrow night there's Indian, Thai, fish and chips, and a Chinese restaurant to choose from.'

Jasper, Felix and Saffy stood with their mouths hanging open.

'Beats the food hall, eh?' Mac said as he grabbed a hot chip.

Jasper leapt towards the table, ignoring the plates and cutlery that Mac had laid out. Felix and Saffy were right behind him.

'This is awesome!' said Saffy.

'It's one of the perks of being on a Hunt,' Mac explained. 'All this helps to fill your body with excitement and happiness. When you feel good, it's a whole lot harder for monsters to tap into any negative feelings. If you had this luxury all the time, it wouldn't seem so good, would it?'

Saffy grunted something through her food. She swallowed, then started again. 'I don't think I would mind, really.'

Mac smiled. 'I already ate, so I'm gonna hit the sack. Don't stay up too late. We have a lot to get through in the morning. I'll wake you up at 6.30am. Try to get some sleep.'

'Six-thirty? That's almost as bad as at school,' groaned Felix.

'No way, I'd take this place over school any day,' said Jasper, cramming some wedges into his mouth. 'Do you reckon we have to go back?'

Saffy winked. 'My thoughts exactly.'

Something told Jasper she wasn't joking.

Jasper woke in the middle of the night with a start. He was terrified. *I am becoming a monster! What if the whispering starts while I'm on the Hunt?*

In a sleepy fog, he stumbled into the kitchen to get a glass of water. He switched on the light.

'Good morning!' a cheery voice boomed.

Jasper jumped. An old man in a plumed helmet was sitting on a horse with a cup of tea in his hand.

'Principal Von Strasser?'

This was seriously weird.

That old guy's weird!

'Up nice and early, I see,' said Von Strasser warmly. 'Good, good. Probably getting in some study before your first big Hunt. Grand.'

Jasper couldn't help wondering how Von Strasser had managed to get inside the kitchen on the horse – and without spilling his tea.

'What time ...?' Jasper managed to mutter.

'It's 3.02am, and twenty-one seconds.' He swung the chain of his pocket watch around in a circle then landed it elegantly back inside his pocket. 'Tea?'

'Ah, no thanks. What are you –? I thought teachers couldn't come on Hunts.'

'Well, technically yes, that is quite true,' conceded Von Strasser. 'But I felt it necessary to bend the rules, having spoken to Señor Hermes about your particular ... situation. I thought perhaps there were some points you'd like resolved before you go on your Hunt.

We can't have you feeling uneasy, it will excite the Glibberhowl. However, I must ask you to be quick. I can only stay for another nine minutes and thirty-nine seconds. Otherwise I may compromise the location of Monstrum House. You never know when a Scrambler is about.'

Jasper was suddenly wide awake. There were a million questions he wanted to ask.

'Do you know what happened? When I was bitten, I mean.'

'It was a nasty event. You were four at the time. You woke in the night for a drink and you stumbled upon a Scrambler who was stalking your younger sister. You leapt to her defence by jumping on the monster's head. In the process, you were bitten. It showed some strength of character, to attack a monster at such an early age. Most four-year-olds would have been terrified.'

'But why can't I remember it? It seems like

the kind of thing I wouldn't forget in a hurry.'

'You were traumatised to say the least. We sent a Memory Modifier to work with you for a while. While posing as your postman, he managed to transform your memory of the incident until it was nothing more than a nightmare. It's what we do in the most serious cases.'

'A Memory Modifier?' Jasper asked.

'Yes, Memory Modification is just one of the careers that Monstrum House sets you up for upon graduation,' said Von Strasser. 'However, that is a rather rare career path. Most, like your mother, do something more closely related to Hunting, such as Tracking and Trailing.'

My mother? Surely Jasper had misheard him. *But Mum is a garbage collector.*

'Not exactly,' said Von Strasser. 'Your mother actually works for our Tracking Department.

She's a Senior Tracker. We provide the garbage truck as a cover. But rather than collecting rubbish, she is actually tracking monsters through dark streets in the early hours. Pretty nifty, no?'

'Tracker?' Jasper whispered in disbelief. For some reason the idea that his mum worked for Monstrum House seemed crazier than the idea that he was becoming a monster. 'Does she know? About me, I mean? And the bite?'

'Of course! That's why she wanted you to go to Monstrum House – to learn how to *use* it.'

'She *wanted* me to go to Monstrum?'

'Well, when you kept getting expelled for mischievous behaviour she could see that your Scrambler side was getting a little out of hand. She knew it was necessary. It's sometimes hard to accept that your children are old enough to be sent out hunting monsters. But she knew you'd love it. She knew you'd be a good hunter.'

'But isn't it a bit strange? You know, *hunting* monsters and *being* one as well?'

'No, not at all. And you're not a monster. Problems only start if your monsterness takes over. But if you learn to control it – as Hermes is teaching you – you'll see how helpful it is.'

Something was still bothering Jasper. 'Principal Von Strasser,' he said. 'Is the buzz I feel when I hunt … OK?'

But before Von Strasser could answer, Felix stumbled into the kitchen, rubbing his eyes.

'What's all the noise?' Felix yawned. He opened his eyes and yelped when he saw Von Strasser.

'We're, er … having a meeting,' said Jasper.

Felix's yell woke Saffy, who looked equally surprised to find their principal on a horse in the kitchen in the middle of the night.

'I thought teachers couldn't come on Hunts,' she said bluntly.

Von Strasser balanced the tea cup on the horse's head, and then reached under his helmet and pulled out a teapot. He refilled his cup and placed the pot back under his hat.

'I am not *on* the Hunt. I am merely having a last-minute tete-a-tete before *you* go on the Hunt. But I have five minutes left, so ... any questions? Now is the time to ask.'

'Yeah, I have one,' said Saffy, looking wide awake. 'What happens to the monsters? After we catch 'em, I mean? Stenka says they can't be killed. So what happens?'

'We change them,' Von Strasser replied. 'You hunters use a monster's weakness to catch it. The weakness stops the monster, so it is no longer an immediate threat. But a caught monster is still a monster, and so it must be changed.'

'Yeah, but how?'

'Yes. How?' Von Strasser looked lost in thought. 'Oh right, well, let me just say that monsterness is emphasised by certain environ-ments,' said Von Strasser. 'Monsters thrive in cold, dark, scary places. If a monster is taken out of this environment for a long period of time, their monster characteristics eventually diminish.'

'So what environment do you put them in?' Saffy persisted.

'There is a room at Monstrum House. We keep it warm and cosy, filled with light, music and general happiness. The monsters are placed in this room and pampered. They are fed well, patted, read to, played with, and so on. And gradually they lose their monsterness. They become ordinary creatures. At this point, they are re-housed back into the community.'

'You mean, back into the *normal* world?' Felix stammered.

'Precisely,' Von Strasser replied. 'When monsters first hatch they are quite ordinary creatures. Perfectly harmless. Their monsterness comes from a plant that they eat when they hatch.'

'Hang on. They hatch from eggs?' asked Saffy. Jasper remembered how Hermes had mentioned that earlier.

'Yes, and, as you may have noticed, monsters are not the most loving creatures. So instead of feeding their young, they leave their eggs in a nest made from a plant that provides all the monsterness their hatchlings need to turn into monsters. The plant is called a birth plant. The monster hatchlings, with nothing else to eat, start eating their nest, which is jam-packed with monsterness. This plant causes them to form monster characteristics. They grow, mutate and become monsters. Quite remarkable.'

'So, you can reverse that?' asked Felix.

'Yes, indeed, Mr Brown. Birth plants grow in the coldest, darkest, least hospitable places. By providing a warm and loving environment, the monster characteristics will lessen, and lie dormant.'

'But what would happen if, like, a person ate the plant?' asked Felix. 'Would they turn into a monster?'

'No,' said Von Strasser. 'There is only one way for people to turn into monsters.'

Jasper's stomach leapt. Felix looked from Jasper to Von Strasser, and back again.

'You don't mean to say it's true?'

'What? What's true?' asked Saffy.

'My brothers told me about these monster-people –' Felix began.

'They are not monster-people,' cut in Von Strasser. 'Rather, people who have been bitten by a monster. And yes, there are many of them. You would never know who they are, because they're fantastically capable of controlling any monsterness. Most find it an advantage when hunting.' Von Strasser didn't even glance at Jasper.

Felix gasped.

Jasper wasn't sure if he'd ever be able to tell his friends his secret. He felt very alone.

'What's the advantage they have?' Saffy asked.

'Well, it greatly improves your monster awareness. The monsterness is excited by contact with monsters. It often will guide the bitten person towards other monsters – which can be an advantage in a Hunt.'

'So … you have to be bitten to be one of these

people, right?' asked Felix, looking nervous.

'Yes,' said Von Strasser with a small smile. 'And *you*, Mr Brown, have been spiked by a Bogglemorph and sucked by a Cranklesucker, but you have not been bitten.' He pulled out his pocket watch. 'I am out of time. And now it is late. I must sleep.' He lay down on his horse and started snoring.

Saffy snorted back a giggle.

'He's seriously weird. What do we do?' Felix whispered.

Von Strasser's hand rose mid-snore and he clicked his fingers. Instantly the lights went off, leaving them in darkness.

Jasper felt his way around the kitchen table and turned on the light. But Von Strasser and his horse were gone.

'Wakey wakey!' Mac chirped.

Jasper felt like he'd only just closed his eyes.

'Noooooo,' Felix moaned, pulling the pillow over his head.

Saffy sighed and pulled the covers up.

Mac walked casually into the bathroom, returning with a bucket.

Jasper leapt out of bed. 'I'm up!' he squealed. He knew what was in the bucket. His mum had found this an effective method of getting him out of bed when he lived at home.

Saffy followed suit. Felix, however, still had the pillow over his head.

'One, two, three!' Mac warned. He pulled the covers back, and tipped the entire bucket of icy-cold water over Felix.

Felix screamed.

Jasper and Saffy rolled about on the floor, laughing.

'Come on – there's breakfast on the table. Then it's time to show you lot around,' Mac grinned, throwing Felix a towel.

Felix's scowl vanished at the mention of breakfast. 'Is it as good as last night's dinner?'

'It *is* last night's dinner,' Mac replied. 'I hope you're in the mood for melted chocolate sundae, because the chips aren't so good cold.'

Jasper frowned at the food on the table. 'I thought we were supposed to have good food to keep us extra happy on the Hunt.'

Mac smiled. 'It's still better than the food back at Monstrum House, and anyway, the only other stuff we have here is some flour and a couple of eggs. But there is some milk for tea or coffee – oooh, I could even do a chocolate milkshake!' Mac grabbed a sundae and started scooping the chocolate sauce off the top.

Saffy grinned. 'Pancakes, anyone?'

Jasper dropped his spoonful of sundae. 'Definitely,' he said.

Felix nodded eagerly. 'Good one,' he said, with his mouth full of sundae.

Mac settled himself down on the couch. 'Right, you start cooking, and I'll go over the plan. Jasper – you'll be the target.'

Jasper wasn't sure he liked the sound of that.

'You'll swim out into the deepest and darkest part of the lake. At dusk. When you get there, pretend to get tired. Try to imagine what it must feel like for a normal kid. Try to feel some fear. But also ... keep a lid on it,' Mac warned.

'The monster will strike when you are at your weakest,' Mac explained. 'It looks for kids who can't swim well, who go out of their depth and then panic.'

'Panic, yep. I'm sure I can do that,' Jasper joked. But no-one laughed.

'As soon as it focuses on you, Felix will be there to get the fire up its nostril. It won't be prepared for two swimmers. Or for an attack. Saffy will be waiting on the shore, and I'll be directing via earpieces from a lookout. Once the flame reaches the Glibberhowl's inner nostril, it will stop it in its tracks. At least, that's the theory. Saffy will have a net waiting to help you drag it back in.'

Saffy stopped whisking the pancakes. 'You want me to just wait on the shore with a net?'

'Yeah, well, that's important,' Mac said. 'We have no idea how big it will be, although Glibberhowls have been known to reach over 100 kilos. Once it's completely out of the water, it will begin to shrivel and shrink. I'll meet you with the sack and the truck. Of course, the tricky thing is figuring out how to get fire up its nose ... Which is why you lot will have to turn stuff from the tip into a James Bond gadget,' Mac grinned. 'I'm going to spend this morning surveying the area, making sure that there's only one monster operating.'

Jasper groaned. It was bad enough having to find a way to catch one monster. Especially when he was worried about controlling his own monster side.

'Great breakfast, Saffy.' Mac dropped his plate

into the sink. 'I will definitely be bringing you on a Hunt again.'

'Don't expect pancakes every time,' she muttered.

Mac grinned. 'Check this out,' he said, and opened the door.

Bright light flooded in through the doorway. They were right on the shore of a lake.

'Is that,' Felix asked incredulously, 'the sun?'

Saffy jumped up from the table and ran outside. 'Well, if we're going to die,' she called back, 'it might as well be here. This is paradise.'

Jasper stepped through the doorway and right onto the banks of the most beautiful lake he had ever seen. The water sparkled invitingly, and the sun beat down on his back. 'Even though I *know* what's in there, I *still* want to jump in.'

Saffy was already dipping her toes in the water that lapped at the bank.

'I can't believe how good the sun feels!' Felix said, ripping off his hoodie.

'And no stupid snow!' Jasper flicked off his shoes and wriggled his feet in the sand.

Jasper gazed out over the water. There were icy peaks in the distance, but the sun was warm. The water looked *so* tempting. He just couldn't imagine anything horrible lurking in there.

'So, that's the lake. Nice, huh? We're not due back for a couple of days, so if we catch the Glibberhowl tonight, then you'll have a whole day to enjoy yourselves,' Mac said.

Jasper smiled just thinking about it. He turned back to Mac, who was standing in the doorway to what looked like a run-down old cabin. The outside didn't match the insides at all. Jasper had to poke his head back inside to make sure

the cabin really was where they were staying.

'I thought we must be in some fancy hotel or something,' Jasper commented.

Mac shook his head. 'Nah, Monstrum House has people who sort out accommodation before the Hunt crew arrives. We don't want to attract attention, and fancy places don't let kids stay by themselves, so we do up old shacks like this one. They don't look like much, but on the inside – pure luxury.'

Jasper wondered if his mum ever did that in her work for Monstrum. She had a lot of explaining to do when he got home. And he'd have a lot to tell her. It was a relief to know he could tell her what he'd been doing, and that she'd believe him. He knew she would be proud that he made it to a Hunt in his first year.

Now all he had to do was survive it.

Jasper and Felix were hunched over a mound of junk. Bits and pieces of wire and plastic stuck up all around them, along with broken toys, bottle tops and an old rubber hose.

Jasper was still annoyed that they weren't allowed to invent outside while taking in some sun and sand. But Mac had pointed out that a group of kids poring over rubbish didn't exactly look normal.

Felix slammed the manual closed. 'Nothing,' he huffed.

'I told you,' Jasper replied. He had already been through the *Functional Fixedness Helpful Hints Handbook,* looking for something that might help them make the gadget they needed. But he couldn't see anything in there.

Saffy stomped through the door, carrying three giant milkshakes, her hunt belt clipped loosely around her waist.

'Good one, although it took you long enough.' Felix grabbed his shake and slurped appreciatively.

Saffy had been gone for almost an hour, and Jasper suspected she may have sneaked off to soak up some sun.

'Yeah, she was trying to impress the other kids by walking around with her hunt belt on,' Jasper teased. Mac had told them to wear their belts all the time, just in case, but they did look kind of stupid. 'And why have you got your hoodie on? And a scarf? Have you forgotten how hot it is out there? We're not at Monstrum House, you know,' Jasper added as he grabbed his milkshake.

'Say hello to Houdini,' Saffy smirked, glancing around the cabin before unwinding her scarf.

'Houdini? Yeah, right. What about the tag?' Jasper replied. 'You know, the one injected into your neck? You escape and I'll kiss your feet.' Jasper shook his head.

Felix was chortling into his milkshake. 'Nah, Saffy's too clever,' Felix joked, 'She's worked out a way of removing her head.'

Jasper and Felix laughed. Saffy didn't.

'Laugh if you will, but while you've been reading that, I've been reading this.' She produced a book from her bag, *Tracking Techniques and Technology*. 'Our tags have got some chip in them that transmits a signal via satellite to a GPS receiver. I'll bet that's the computer in Stenka's office. So all we have to do is block the signal, and they can't track us.'

'Good plan. But how can we block something that's inside our necks?' asked Felix.

'With this.' Saffy took her scarf off completely.

Jasper burst out laughing, snorting milkshake out his nose. Saffy had tinfoil wrapped tightly around her neck.

She flipped down her hood, ignoring Jasper's snorts. 'If a GPS device is covered in metal, a satellite can't read its signal. Foil should do the trick,' she explained.

Jasper wiped the milkshake from his nose and shook his head at Saffy. She couldn't be serious. But Jasper had never seen Saffy look so pleased with herself.

She's serious all right, Jasper thought. *She's also nuts.* Jasper didn't even want to think about

Saffy's new scarf
You're being watched
Beep, beep, beep...
Foil layer
Chip
Scarf

what Stenka might do to Saffy if – no, *when* –
she was caught.

'And I have more foil for you guys.' She
pointed at her backpack. 'All we do is wrap you
up, and we are home free.' Saffy chuckled like
some sort of evil genius.

'There's no way it'll work,' said Jasper.

Saffy shrugged.'Suit yourself.'

'Couldn't you have put your brain to
something useful?' Jasper asked. 'Like helping
us find a way to shoot fire up a monster's nose
while it's *under* water?' He pointed to the junk
surrounding them.

'You mean you still haven't figured anything
out?' said Saffy.

Felix looked annoyed. 'At least we've been
trying,' he muttered.

Saffy shook her head and sighed. 'Do I have
to do everything myself? Try this.' She leant

over and grabbed a rubber hose. 'Add this,' she sifted through the rubbish until she found an old jack-in-the-box. She pulled the head off the bouncing clown and handed Jasper the spring. 'Now, use this bit of rope as a fuse, then a firelighter as ammunition. Seal it so it's watertight, then stick it up the monster's nose and *kapow*.'

Jasper just stared. *Why didn't we think of that?*

'I'm out of here,' Saffy said, heading towards the door.

'What about the Hunt?' Felix asked.

Jasper looked at Saffy. 'Yeah, he's right. What about catching the Glibberhowl? Protecting everyone from the monster? What about ... us?'

Saffy stopped and glared at them. 'You two are fine. You heard Stenka, what use am I if I can't even swim? And all Mac thinks I'm good at is holding a net and making pancakes! It's fine for you two. Jasper, your mum was a student, so they'll keep you. Felix, you're a Brown Brother, so you're set. But *I'm* the one who has to *prove* myself. You heard what Stenka said. I might not be *able* to come back. I *can't* swim. And there's no way I'm going back to being shunted around by my parents like a piece of luggage. I've gotta do my own thing. This is my chance.'

'Holding a net is important,' Felix said. 'I'd happily hold a net.'

'And there's no way Stenka won't let you come back. You're one of the best students in our year,' Jasper added.

'Yeah right,' said Saffy.

'Come on, Saffy,' Jasper pleaded.

But Saffy was beyond reasoning. 'I'll see ya.' She waved, spun on her heel and left.

'Come on, Felix! Hurry up!' yelled Jasper as he raced to the shore.

Felix was dragging his feet through the sand. He wasn't as excited as Jasper was about starting the Hunt.

When Jasper got to the shore he tore open his backpack. 'The FlameShooter 6000,' he whispered. He was pretty pleased with himself.

Well, OK, Felix had a bit to do with making it, Jasper thought. *And without Saffy, we probably wouldn't have it at all. But still, I thought of the name.*

'And now to see if it works,' Jasper said out loud. 'Felix, hurry up!'

Felix was glancing nervously at the lake. 'It's late afternoon. Almost dusk,' he said uneasily.

'And?' Jasper rolled his eyes. The sun was shining brightly and the banks were still crowded – not a thing to worry about.

'But Mac said it likes attacking at dusk,' Felix argued.

Jasper shook his head and shoved Felix towards the lake. 'Don't be soft. Monsters only attack in the dark. We're just going to test the FlameShooter 6000 in the shallows, then take it back to Mac. The poor guy needs something to cheer him up.'

Mac had spent the last three hours storming up and down the house, using Saffy's name in sentences which really weren't very nice. He swore she wouldn't actually be able to escape,

126

no matter what her plan. But Jasper could tell he was worried. Apparently, no hunt captain in the history of Monstrum House had ever lost a crew member. Other than those who had died horrible deaths during a Hunt.

No-one had ever escaped from a Hunt before, either. No-one had even *tried* to escape. Mac didn't know whether to tell Stenka or not. From what Jasper could make out from Mac's ramblings, Saffy would be safer if she never came back.

'Come on,' grinned Jasper, trying to make Felix feel better. 'We'll test out the FlameShooter 6000, cheer up Mac, and convince him to treat us to something special for dinner. Something to make Saffy jealous. Chances are she'll come back starving and miserable.'

Felix seemed slightly cheered up by this thought. But Jasper was trying not to think about the possibility that they might never see Saffy again. He was furious with her, and at the same time really worried. *Keep busy, and don't think about it,* he told himself.

Jasper opened the box and took out their invention. It was perfect. It was a sealed rubber hose with a spring inside it. Using the waterproof matches from his hunt belt, Jasper would light the fuse at one end of the hose. The fuse took exactly thirty-one seconds to reach the ammunition – a firelighter weighed down with lead to help propel it. As soon as the firelighter caught on fire, Jasper just had to shove the tube up the monster's nose and release the spring to catapult it up the left nostril. He would have to get the timing just right. This was going to be tricky.

At the edge of the lake, Jasper put the

The FlameShooter 6000

Waterproof match

Spring trigger

Fuse

6000

Seal

Firelighter

Spring

Slingshot

Seal

Firelighter shoots out of tube...

FlameShooter 6000 on top of the water and smiled. 'Test one. It floats!'

'No leaks,' Felix confirmed, inspecting the seals. He looked at the water and nervously fingered his hunt belt.

Jasper thought guiltily of his own hunt belt dumped on the floor of the cabin, but there was no way he was walking around in broad daylight with a mini toilet-plunger hanging from his waist. He just hoped Mac didn't notice that he wasn't wearing it.

Jasper stepped into the lake, up to his ankles. The water was the most brilliant blue he had ever seen. Even the pebbles looked blue. He scooped some water into his hands and splashed it over his head and face.

'Ahhh, that's better,' he sighed. He squinted into the glare from the sun, and wondered if Mac had brought any sunglasses. Jasper stood back up, feeling slightly dizzy.

Guess I'm not used to so much sun, he thought. Almost a whole year in freezing weather was obviously having an effect on him.

Jasper looked longingly at the water. His whole body was urging him to dive in.

'Surely a quick dip would be OK?' he muttered under his breath.

'*YEEESSS*,' Felix whispered behind him.

'Really?' Jasper asked Felix in surprise.

Felix looked at him suspiciously. 'What? I didn't say anything. But Mac said no swimming.'

'Yeah, yeah,' Jasper smiled. The water lapped temptingly at his feet. 'But you know we really need to test the FlameShooter 6000 in the deep. I mean, if everything goes according to plan, we'll be shooting the flame up the tube and into the monster's nostril. That means we'll have to pull it under the water and shoot upwards.

We need to get deep enough to test it.'

Felix was shaking his head wildly from side to side.

But Jasper was convinced that they needed to test the FlameShooter. Otherwise the plan could go all wrong. And that wasn't something he was keen on. Especially as Jasper was the one being used as bait.

Felix was still shaking his head. 'Don't be stupid. Let's get Mac and –'

Jasper grabbed the FlameShooter 6000 from Felix and headed deeper into the water. 'You worry too much,' he grinned. 'Everything will be fine. I'll only go knee-deep.'

Jasper waded further into the water and stared up at the sun. *So good,* he thought. He was feeling great.

'Jasper!' Felix called anxiously from the bank.

Jasper realised that he had walked further

out than he meant to. The water was already up to his chest. And it felt *awesome*.

Jasper couldn't remember the last time he'd been swimming. He lifted his feet and took a few strokes, holding tightly to the FlameShooter. The feeling of weightlessness was fantastic. Jasper dived under the water, letting his breath out slowly. It was like a whole underwater world.

Jaa ... speer ... yessss ....

Jasper shot towards the surface, his heart hammering.

KOOOD ... JAAAA ... SPPEER, KOOOM ...

He wished he'd had more classes with Señor Hermes. Jasper closed his eyes. He tried to see a blank piece of paper. He tried to think of the letters. He could hear his name, but he couldn't understand the other words.

But in the end he gave up trying to see the

words, and focused instead on staying calm. He *didn't* want panic. He floated on his back and tried to breathe deeply, thinking of Christmas and birthdays and anything nice.

The whispering stopped.

Jasper turned and waved to Felix. Felix waved back.

Jasper treaded water, glancing at the bank. He was somehow further out than he had thought. Much further out. His toes couldn't touch the bottom anymore.

Felix was still waving. And suddenly, the thought of all things nice didn't work so well for Jasper. He realised Felix wasn't waving a friendly 'how are you doing' kind of wave. This was more of a frantic 'get back to the shore NOW' kind of wave.

Keep calm, Jasper thought. He knew he was a strong swimmer. And he wasn't *that* far out. He started swimming back towards the shore.

As he stroked through the water, Jasper couldn't help noticing how quickly the sky had darkened. Surely he hadn't been out here for *that* long? Or had he? Jasper felt as though he'd lost all track of time. He found himself squinting to make out the bank. He couldn't see Felix anywhere. His eyes felt tired and sore.

Jasper started swimming more frantically,

trying to keep his breathing even, trying to keep his fear under control. With every stroke Jasper felt as though he was getting further and further away from the bank. He looked up. He *was* getting further away from the bank. His head felt fuzzy from all the swimming. He desperately tried to keep images of the Glibberhowl out of his head. But it wasn't working.

Jasper felt a cold prickle of fear run over his scalp. He froze, feeling something stirring in the water beneath him. And if it was the same something he thought it was, then fear was the very worst thing for Jasper to be feeling.

The water around him swirled, sucking downwards, like he was caught in a whirlpool. Jasper felt something slimy sweep past his leg. He started swimming again as fast as he could towards the shore. He forced himself to take deep, rhythmic breaths as he pounded through the water. *Just a fish, just a fish, keep calm, keep in control,* Jasper said to himself.

But Jasper *knew* it wasn't a fish. It was the Glibberhowl. And *he* was the victim.

Just as planned, he thought, *except for the 'no-one to help, all on my own' bit.*

Jasper swam fiercely as the monster swept past again. He could see its dark shadow beneath him. He could see it coming towards him.

The swirling current pulled him closer and closer to the Glibberhowl. *Not if I can help it.* Jasper kicked his legs harder, but he couldn't get away. He gripped the FlameShooter tightly.

Jasper felt something slimy wrap around his leg and pull him down. He turned to see a wall of mud rising out of the water. A small, green eye peered excitedly from the thick, brown mucousy slime, looking straight at Jasper. He could just make out two black nostrils.

Glibberhowl

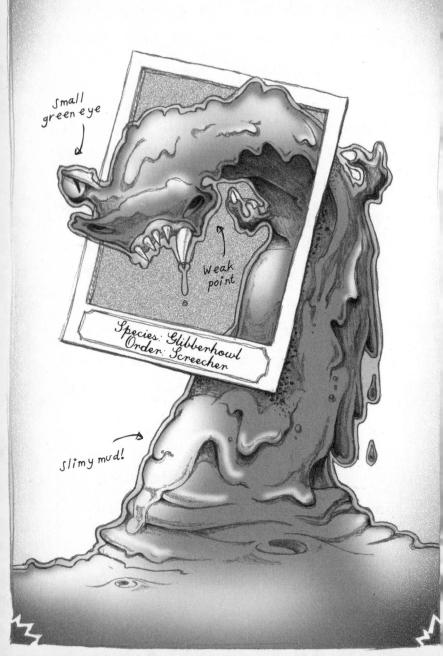

It comes out of the water to attack! Jasper thought helplessly. He wondered if he would ever get the chance to tell Mac.

Jasper tried to aim the FlameShooter, but he wasn't wearing his hunt belt and he realised he had no way to light the fuse. He kicked his legs, but they were covered in slime. He shut down his mind, refusing to let himself panic, refusing to let the monster grow bigger.

But then it had him. The Glibberhowl slurped at him, then dived. Jasper felt himself being sucked under.

He took one last deep lungful of air before he was pulled down into the dark watery depths.

Jasper's lungs were burning. He couldn't hold his breath for much longer. He was going to die. How had this happened?

Then his head filled with whispering again.

PREEETTY SCRRAMBLLEEEERRS!

A blank piece of paper popped into Jasper's head. The words crossed themselves out until he saw exactly what the whispering was saying.

Scramblers! he thought. *There are Scramblers!*

He remembered Mac saying he needed to survey the area for other monster species. He remembered how blue the pebbles had looked at the bottom of the lake. *They must have been Scramblers, not pebbles.* Jasper realised why everything had gone so wrong. Now it was beginning to make sense – the confusion, the sore eyes, the dizziness. He had been Scrambled. Again! Stupid Scramblers!

Jasper wasn't feeling scared anymore, just determined. He knew what he had to do. To get the Scramblers out, he needed to blow his nose as hard as he could. If only he had enough breath left to blow with. But Jasper's lungs were empty.

He kicked strongly against the Glibberhowl. He had to get to the surface.

Then strong hands gripped Jasper from above. He looked up to see Felix's neatly nose-pegged and ear-plugged face above him, pulling him towards the surface of the lake. There was a furious swirling of water, and then the Glibberhowl released Jasper's legs and moved silently away.

No way, Jasper thought. He kicked as hard as he could towards the surface. His lungs were screaming in pain.

Felix wrenched Jasper upwards until his head broke through the surface of the water. He didn't know air could taste so good. He gasped in the cool night breeze, choking and spluttering.

Jasper didn't wait to become confused again.

He blew his nose as hard as he could. A bright blue Scrambler shot out of his nostril, covered in snot. Instantly Jasper's head cleared. He'd just have to keep his head above water, so no more Scramblers could get in. *I really wish I had my earplugs now,* he thought.

Jasper gave Felix the thumbs up. 'Thanks, I seriously owe you one,' he rasped, as they treaded water in the middle of the lake.

Felix didn't look so pleased. 'Did you see it? It was *huge!* And its eye! A horrible green!' Felix sounded terrified.

'No, no, calm down. It's gone!' Jasper said. The last thing they needed was for the Glibberhowl to come back now.

But it was too late. The Glibberhowl had slimed itself around Felix's leg and was pulling him under. Jasper tried to grab hold of Felix, but the monster was too strong. In seconds

Felix was gone.

'FELIX!' Jasper screamed desperately.

The sound of a boat's motor roared towards him. Jasper turned to see a speedboat hurtling through the water, with Saffy at the wheel and Mac behind her.

'Saffy!' cried Jasper. The boat swerved to a stop next to him.

'Got ya!' Mac reached into the water and pulled him up into the boat.

'It's got Felix!' Jasper screamed. Felix wouldn't be able to hold his breath for long at all. He had asthma attacks at the best of times.

Mac's jaw dropped open. 'Where? When?' he shouted.

Jasper pointed. He was still clinging to the FlameShooter. Saffy was throwing off her shoes, getting ready to jump in. But Jasper knew *he* was the only one who had a chance.

143

He grabbed a box of matches, popped the seal off the FlameShooter 6000, and lit the fuse.

Thirty-one seconds. Jasper sealed the tube again to keep it water-tight, shoved some plugs in his ears and nose and leapt into the water. *Thirty-one seconds before the firelighter catches alight.*

Jasper swam further and further under the water. But he couldn't see anything.

And then he realised that he was relying on the wrong sense. Jasper closed his eyes and listened.

YESSS!

Jasper had no idea where he was swimming, but he knew the whispering would lead him towards the monster. He just had to follow it. He felt excitement creep up inside him, and for the first time since Jasper had learnt about the whispering, he was pleased to have it.

YEEESSSS!! HEERE!

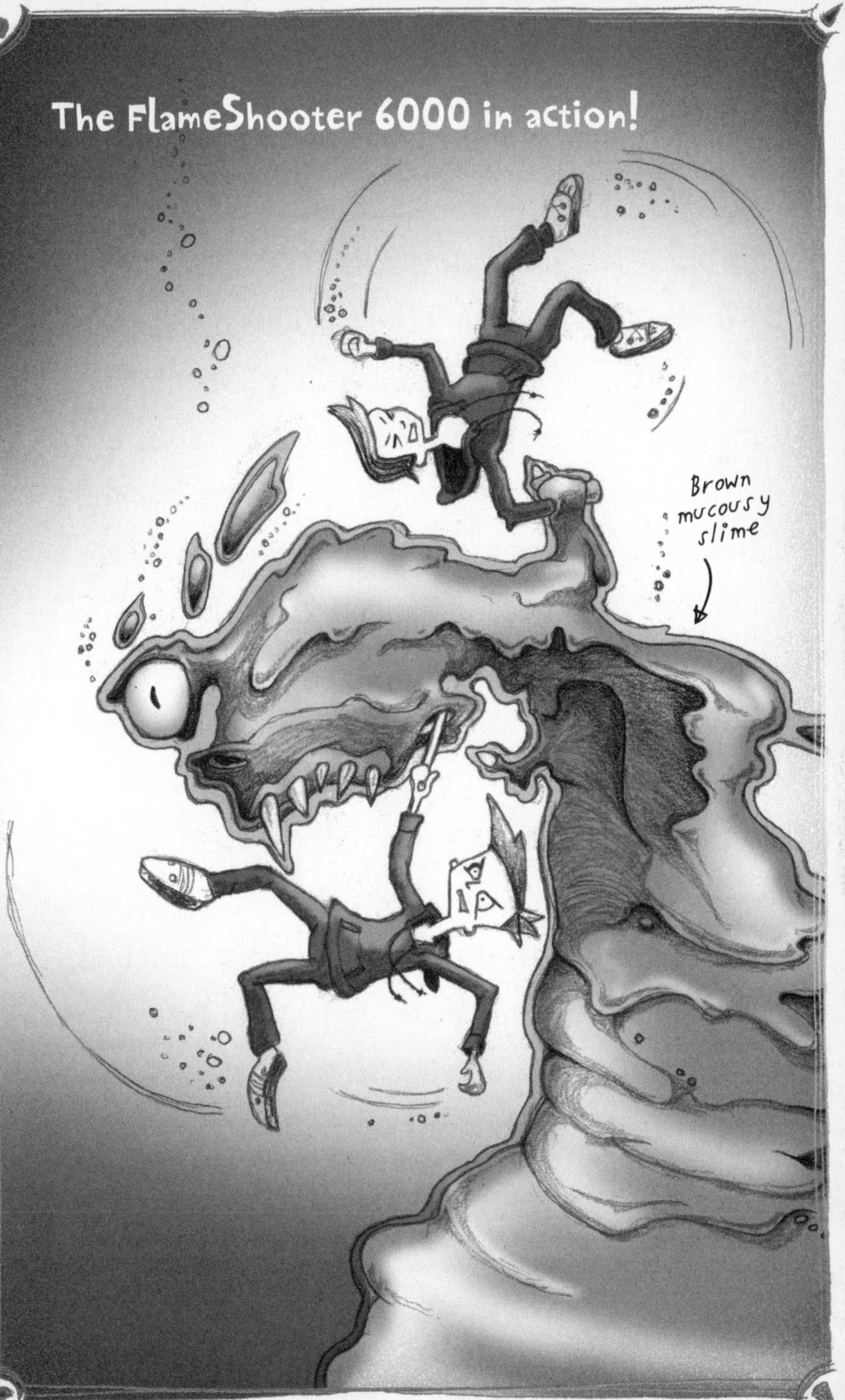
The FlameShooter 6000 in action!
Brown mucousy slime

Jasper opened his eyes. Felix was directly in front of him. He could see the fear spread across his friend's face. And he could see the Glibberhowl growing bigger before his eyes. It was feeding on Felix's fear, its body bubbling out more and more thick slimy mud. The monster's green eye was half closed in intense pleasure. But Jasper knew it wouldn't keep feeding for long – Felix couldn't hold his breath forever.

Thirty-one seconds were up. Jasper took aim. He heard a *whoosh* as the firelighter inside caught alight. He stuffed the FlameShooter up the Glibberhowl's left nostril, then flicked the trigger.

The Glibberhowl's green eye popped open in horror. And then it froze. Jasper just had time to see Felix's look of relief before Mac appeared, and pulled them both towards the surface.

Jasper stared uneasily at the telephone. Mac had sent a hunt report back to Stenka, and now Stenka wanted to speak to Jasper.

'She's going to be pleased, yeah?' said Jasper hopefully. 'I mean, we did catch the Glibberhowl. She's got to be glad about that, right?' But he wasn't feeling so sure.

'This is Stenka, remember,' said Mac. 'She'll be pleased we got the monster – but I had to report *everything* that happened. I couldn't leave out the fact you went swimming with Scramblers.'

'So how come you didn't put in the bit about Saffy escaping in your report, then?' Jasper whinged.

'Well, that's different,' said Mac. 'Can you imagine what Stenka would do? Escaping from a Hunt is *unthinkable* at Monstrum House. If she hadn't come back ...' he trailed off. 'I'm saving her skin, you know? And mine,' he added. 'Anyway, I reckon you deserve to get into trouble. Next time, you can test your underwater inventions in the bath.'

Jasper supposed Mac was right. And Mac had already had it out with Saffy. 'Stenka always gives that speech about proving yourself to someone on a new crew,' Mac had yelled at Saffy. 'It's supposed to make you determined to prove what you've got. It's not supposed to make you nick off!'

Jasper looked at Saffy sitting there, munching

on a chocolate bar. 'Just 'cos you managed to weasel your way out of it,' he mumbled, wishing he'd been as lucky.

'Weasel?' Saffy replied indignantly. 'Just remember, *I* was watching. If it wasn't for me hot-wiring the boat and finding Mac, you two would be fish food.'

There wasn't any point arguing, especially as Saffy was right. He *hated* it when Saffy was right.

Felix walked into the room. 'Has she called yet?' he asked chirpily, heading over to the fridge for a chocolate bar.

Jasper moaned and shook his head.

'She will. She's just making you sweat it out a bit.' Mac sucked on a lollipop thoughtfully. 'I wonder what your punishment will be.'

'But I got the monster, didn't I?' Jasper said weakly.

'Yeah, but you also went into *known* monster

territory without your hunt belt on. Even Saffy took hers, and she was escaping!' Mac said.

'OK, OK, I get it,' Jasper groaned. He got the feeling Mac was enjoying this.

'There's no chocolate left!' Felix complained from behind the fridge door.

Saffy shook her head. 'Don't even think about it,' she said, just as Felix made a lunge for her chocolate bar.

Mac leant over and looked closely at Jasper. 'Seriously, though, it was good work to let yourself be guided. You kept control of the whispering beautifully,' he said quietly.

Jasper froze. 'How do you …?'

Mac glanced up at the others. Saffy and Felix were still fighting over the last chocolate bar and weren't taking any notice. 'It's a bit freaky at first, but once you get your head around it, it's actually pretty cool. It's like having an

150

internal monster compass. You just have to show it who's boss.'

Jasper was stunned. *Mac! A Whispered?*

'You can kiss my ...' Saffy squirmed out of Felix's reach, then shoved the last bit of chocolate into her mouth. 'Which reminds me,' Saffy turned to Jasper. 'Which foot do you want to kiss first?'

Felix burst out laughing.

'You said that if I escaped, you would kiss my feet,' she reminded Jasper sweetly.

'No way! It doesn't count! You came back!' Jasper said indignantly.

Saffy stood up and started towards him. 'That's only because I had to rescue you,' she smiled smugly. 'I could've been long gone.'

Jasper turned to Mac for support, but he just laughed.

'She does have a point,' said Mac. 'Plus she's

got a cool idea for getting rid of the Scramblers in the lake. You better find your earplugs and nosepegs.' He wandered out of the room.

Jasper was really looking forward to enjoying a nice relaxing swim in that lake. He hoped the plan was a quick one. Or one that consisted of Jasper lolling on the water while everyone else caught the monsters.

Saffy flicked Jasper with her towel. 'Come on, where's your hunt belt?'

'Weren't you planning to escape more permanently?' asked Jasper.

'What, and let you lot try to handle things?' Saffy snorted. 'I don't think so!'

Felix rolled his eyes. 'And I thought we'd finally got rid of her.'

The phone began to ring. Felix and Saffy looked at Jasper.

'Saved by the bell. Enjoy,' Saffy whispered,

but she looked quite sympathetic.

Felix patted him on the back. 'Tough one, mate,' he said quietly.

Jasper plucked up his courage, and picked up the phone. 'H-h-hello?' he said, trying not to sound nervous.

'Got ya,' said Mac on the other end. He was calling from the other room.

'Mac!' groaned Jasper. 'She's going to ring any minute!'

'No, she won't. I didn't say a word,' he said.

Jasper couldn't believe it. 'But – I thought you had to report *everything*?'

'I was just winding you up,' said Mac. 'What happens on a Hunt, stays on a Hunt.'

Jasper smiled and hung up the phone. Mac popped his head around the door. 'I wouldn't look too relieved,' he warned. 'You haven't heard Saffy's plan yet.'

'He makes such good bait,' Jasper heard Saffy say from the other room.

'Bait?' said Jasper. 'No way, Saffy. I'm not being bait again! It's your turn! Safy? Saffy?!'

TO BE CONTINUED...

Think of a wasp, crossed with a monster. What do you get? A giant killer bug with a sting that makes disgusting pus-filled hives pop up all over your body.

Jasper and his friends have to risk their lives – and their looks – to stop a swarm of these insect-monsters nesting in Monstrum House. They're going to need more than a can of fly spray to beat these bugs!

www.monstrumhouse.com